Murder
and the
First Lady

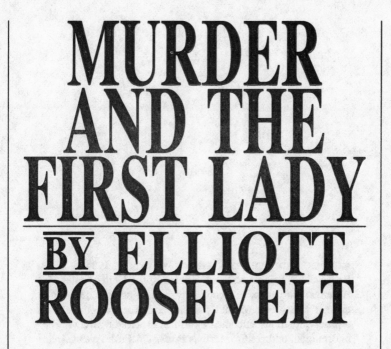

MURDER AND THE FIRST LADY

BY ELLIOTT ROOSEVELT

St. Martin's Press • New York

To my best friend,
my wife Patty

Murder and the First Lady

1

The elevator doors opened. The President of the United States, with quick, powerful thrusts of his arms and shoulders, rolled his wood-and-steel wheelchair out of the elevator and into the second-floor center hall of the White House.

"Who's home?" he boomed exuberantly.

Followed by his black valet but propelling the wheelchair himself, he rolled west along the corridor, into the private sitting room. When he turned and looked back, he could see the length of the long corridor, all the way past the Lincoln Bedroom to the window at the east end of the house. He could see Missy coming—Marguerite Le-Hand, who had been his personal and private secretary for almost twenty years. She hurried along the corridor toward the sitting room, a handsome woman wearing high heels and a form-fitting blue dress. She smiled as her eyes caught his.

"Everything is ready, Mr. President," said the valet as he pushed the wheeled cocktail table close. "The ice. Chilled glasses . . ."

"Oh, that's marvelous, Arthur," said the President. "Thank you. See who's around, will you?"

The valet stood aside at the door as Missy entered, then hurried off down the corridor. Missy walked to the President's side, bent down, and kissed him on the cheek. He patted her hand, affectionately. Already his attention was fixed on the cocktail shaker, the bucket of ice, and the bottles of vermouth and gin.

"Harry's in the house somewhere, I think," he said to Missy.

"I'm sure he is." She sat down on the couch, with her back to the window.

"Harry the Hop," said the President as he pulled the cork from a bottle of Cinzano vermouth. "Wouldn't miss a martini, would he?"

"Only for a good cause," said Missy.

"He and my wife can define a million things as good causes," joked the President. "I hereby proclaim *this*"—nodding at the shaker and the bottles—"a good cause."

He poured vermouth from the bottle into a shot glass, eyeing the liquid critically. Then he poured the vermouth from the glass into a tall silver shaker and began pouring gin into the glass. He was precise, filling the shot glass to exactly the same line each time, mixing his gin and vermouth with the concentration of a pharmacist compounding a medicine. Seven to one was his ratio—seven shots of gin, one of vermouth. With tongs he added ice. Then he pushed the lid down and began to shake.

With a small fork, Missy put olives in two glasses.

"Be nice if we could put the Congress in a shaker with some ice," said the President. *"And shake!"* He shook the martinis vigorously. He laughed.

"They ought to go home," said Missy. "Hot weather is bad for them. Senators wilt in a Washington summer."

The President continued shaking. The silver container was soon beaded with condensation.

"Ah. Here's Harry."

Harry Hopkins came toward them through the hall. A tall, thin, tense man, he hurried.

The President poured a martini into each of the chilled stem glasses. "Harry," he said, handing a glass up to Hopkins. "Have a sip of the nectar."

Hopkins sank gratefully onto the couch, on the end farthest from Missy. He reached for an ashtray and crushed out his cigarette. "Stalin—" he said.

The President interrupted him with a raised hand. "—could curdle a good martini with a glance," he finished. "Let him stew for the hour, Harry. We're entitled to one hour a day without Stalin or Hitler . . . or John L. Lewis."

Missy used the tongs to put ice in a squat glass, and she poured Haig & Haig to fill the glass. She took a grateful sip.

Hopkins, who was tired, slumped on the couch. "I saw a newsreel last night," he said. "Lou Gehrig making his farewell speech in Yankee Stadium." He shook his head and took a sip from his martini. "It was moving. Moving . . ."

"We sent him a note," said the President.

"We've had a letter from the king," said Missy.

"Oh, yes," said the President. "King George. You know, Harry, I think they did have a good time here, official visit and all." He grinned. "I'll never forget that picnic. The king's first hot dog. 'It's quite good, my dear,' he said to the queen. I don't know if he really thought so, or not."

"Your mother was so honored," said Missy. "To have the King and Queen of England as guests in her house . . ."

"Mother was pleased," said the President. "She could even laugh at those wild men from Chicago and their Anglophobe outbursts."

"We don't have much time to overcome that kind of silliness," said Hopkins, closing his eyes and pressing his fingers to the sides of his nose. "Hitler will invade Poland before the weather in Eastern Europe turns and his army can't move. Poland will collapse. Then it will be left to France and England to save Europe—and the question will be: will we stand by them?"

"You know the answer, Harry," said the President.

"We can't let the British fall prey to Hitler," said Missy. "Where, after all, would we get Haig & Haig, or Beefeaters? What would civilization amount to without Scotch whisky and London dry gin?"

The President laughed heartily, and Hopkins, conscious that the President really wanted to banish grim talk, chuckled and nodded. Both of them were indebted to Missy LeHand, who had once more demonstrated her talent for interjecting the light note when they needed it. She clasped the President's arm for a moment, exchanged a private glance with him, and saw him relax.

"Babs," said the President—referring to Mrs. Roosevelt—"is going to take in *The Man Who Came to Dinner* while she's in New York."

"I'd like to get up there and see it," said Hopkins.

"Sometimes I feel like that man myself," said the President. "I came here for dinner, and here I am, still. The difference is, no one would ever voluntarily stay in the White House after he'd had one dinner here—not as long as Mrs. Nesbitt is doing the cooking."

They talked on. Captain McIntyre, the President's doctor, stopped in after a while and accepted a martini. The President was mixing a fresh batch when the telephone rang. Missy answered.

"I'm terribly sorry," she said to the President. "I think you may want to take this call."

With a great show of reluctance, the President put down the cocktail shaker and accepted the telephone from her hand.

"Mr. President," said the voice on the line. "This is Bailey, Secret Service. Sorry to bother you, but I'm afraid I have awkward news. It seems a member of the White House staff has been murdered."

"Who?" asked the President apprehensively.

"A minor member, sir. I'm not sure you're even aware of his name. Philip Garber. He worked for the chief usher."

"I'm aware of his name," said the President. "He's the son of a congressman. Worked downstairs. Right? But only recently."

"He was employed by the chief usher about two months ago, sir," said Bailey. "A bookkeeper, working on the household accounts for the White House."

"What are the circumstances?"

"Well, sir, unfortunately, he's been found dead in the apartment of one of Mrs. Roosevelt's secretaries. The English girl."

"Pamela Rush-Hodgeborne?"

"Yes, sir. I'm afraid, Mr. President, the D.C. police are about to charge her with murdering him."

"What! How?"

"They say he died of poison, something put in a drink he had at her apartment. The girl has admitted she mixed him the drink."

"*Why,* for heaven's sake? Why would she do it?"

"I have no idea, sir. They are holding her for questioning."

"Where are you, Bailey?"

"Police headquarters, sir. They called us as soon as they learned it was a member of the White House staff who'd been killed."

"Well, stay there, Bailey. Stay on it and let me know what develops."

"They've asked if you have any special request in the matter," said Bailey.

"What? Because they're White House people? Only to be sure they're right before they charge that girl with murder. I'd hate to have them compound the tragedy through carelessness."

"Right, sir. I'll stay here and will call again."

The President sighed and shook his head as he put down the telephone. He explained what he had heard.

"Pamela Rush-Hodgeborne . . ." Missy mused. "Pretty little thing. Veddy, veddy English. It's hard to believe she could have killed a man. I'll go so far as to say I don't think I do believe it."

"Garber," said Hopkins, frowning. "Frank Garber's son?"

The President nodded. "A chip off the old block, too, from what little I've observed." He began again to shake his martinis. "Boss Garber will want little Pamela's neck in a noose if it appears she actually did kill his son. Lucky she's not in New Jersey."

"Why was Frank Garber's son working in the White House?" asked Hopkins.

"Oh, Jim arranged it," said the President. "I don't remember the details, but Frank called and asked Jim to fix up something so the boy could work here. Look good for him, I suppose. Jim wanted to accommodate Garber, and yet he didn't want the son where he would have a finger on anything. He put him with the usher. The boy was supposed to be figuring out why it costs so much for food around here— or why we can't have edible food for what we spend."

"Seriously," said Missy, "the Garber boy was a qualified bookkeeper. He was digging through the bills from the days of Hoover. Food, maintenance, staff wages . . . everything."

"God, you don't suppose he found something that . . . ?" Hopkins asked.

"He found out that the Secret Service staff eat out of the White House food budget even though they have a meals allowance from the Treasury budget," said the President. "Of course, I've known that for five years. It's been a perquisite of theirs, it seems. But he wasn't killed for anything like that."

"Maybe someone getting at Frank Garber?" Hopkins suggested.

"Let's hope not," said the President. "Spare me a political scandal, even if Philip Garber was just a bookkeeper in the usher's office."

"Philip and Pamela were, I think, more than just friends," said Missy.

"Jealous lover, then?" asked Captain McIntyre.

"Not impossible," said Missy.

"Where did Mrs. Roosevelt find her?" Hopkins asked.

The President poured fresh martinis into their glasses. "Pamela is a nice girl, according to Babs. She came to this country about three or four months ago, in the entourage of the Countess of Crittenden. The countess brought two of her children for a short tour of the States, and Pamela came along as their tutor."

"Their nanny?"

"No," said the President. "Tutor. Anyway, they spent a weekend at Hyde Park. It seems the earl's father was once a friend of my mother, and the countess had met Babs somewhere, sometime. So Babs invited them, and they came. Pamela made quite an impression, it seems, and Babs offered her a job on her staff here in the White House. The countess was all for the girl staying, said it would be a wonderful experience for her. It was in April, I think, when Pamela went to work for Babs. She was to stay a year, I believe was the deal. I've seen her only a few times, actually. I can tell you, though, Harry —she's a dish. Peaches-and-cream and all that."

"Is she on the government payroll?" Hopkins asked.

The President glanced inquiringly at Missy.

"She's on Mrs. Roosevelt's personal payroll," said Missy. "Officially, she works on Mrs. Roosevelt's newspaper column."

"I'm glad to hear that," said Hopkins.

"It's difficult to think of Pamela Rush-Hodgeborne poisoning Philip Garber," said the President thoughtfully.

"Don't involve yourself," warned Hopkins. "It could be a hot potato."

The President nodded and thoughtfully lifted his glass.

After his valet had helped him with his bath, the President dressed in pajamas and had his dinner tray brought to him in his bedroom. He sat propped up comfortably against two fat pillows and ate from the tray on his lap. Missy, in a light blue nightgown, sat on the foot of the bed and took her dinner from another tray. It was their routine of many years.

"My thoughts keep going back to that girl," said the President. "What an ordeal she's enduring! The poor child is probably in jail by now, unless they've found her innocent already."

"If Mrs. Roosevelt were here, she'd be over at police headquarters," said Missy.

"She'll be there in the morning, you can be sure," said the President. "As soon as she hears about it."

"The morning papers will be full of the story," said Missy.

"Yes. I wish I could keep Babs away from the whole thing. If she could help the girl in any way, I would want her to, of course. But I can do without the publicity she'll generate."

Missy smiled. "I'm afraid you don't have the option," she said quietly.

They listened to the radio news on the hour. The death of Philip Garber had still not impressed itself on the reporters, and the story was not mentioned. Missy put a stack of records on the Victrola inside the radio cabinet, and the muted tones of a Dvořák symphony afforded a pleasant background to their conversation.

They talked more about the recent visit of King George VI and Queen Elizabeth. Missy had been impressed by the regal bearing of the queen, by her furs and jewels. She had found the king "an engaging little chap." The President laughed at that and added that the king would be a shy, likeable man in any circumstance.

The telephone rang.

"Bailey," said Missy, handing over the telephone.

The President put aside his cigarette and holder. "Yes, Bailey," he said. "What news?"

"Very odd, Mr. President," said the voice on the line. "Very odd, I'm afraid—and distressing."

"Indeed?"

"Yes, sir. When they brought her in—Pamela Rush-Hodgeborne, I mean—everyone was inclined to be sympathetic toward her. She *is* a pretty little thing, Mr. President."

"Yes, Bailey. I had noticed that."

"Yes, sir. Well, at my suggestion they notified the British Embassy that they had a British subject in custody and under suspicion for a very serious crime. The embassy sent a legal officer over immediately, and he's been here all along. At the same time, the embassy seems to have wired London, telling them about this matter. About fifteen minutes ago the embassy received a very odd—a very distressing—wire. It seems, sir, that Pamela is not the innocent girl we had thought. Scotland Yard regards her as a principal suspect in a major jewel theft that took place in England last winter."

"Oh, dear."

"Yes, sir. But that's not all of it. It seems, too, that Scotland Yard regards Philip Garber as another principal suspect."

"Garber? But how could that be?"

"Well, sir, Garber spent about a year in England and returned from there in the spring of this year. It seems that both he and Miss Pamela Rush-Hodgeborne were employed on the household staff of the Earl of Crittenden, and—"

"She was a tutor in the earl's household," the President interrupted.

"Yes, sir. And Philip Garber worked for the earl as a bookkeeper— doing the same kind of work he was doing at the White House. Seems he was something of a cad, as Scotland Yard put it. He is known to have had some unsavory associations in London. Anyway, he was suspected in the jewel theft, and so was Pamela. Scotland Yard regards it as a suspicious circumstance that Philip left the earl's employ shortly after the theft and six months later he and Pamela wound up working together and seeing each other in Washington."

"Just how close were Pamela and Philip?" the President asked.

"Well, sir . . . they spent the night together from time to time, in her apartment. The relationship was not innocent, sir."

"How unfortunate," said the President.

"Congressman Garber has been here, sir," said Bailey unhappily.

"I suppose so," said the President. "And?"

"Earlier he was demanding the firmest possible action against the young lady. When he was told his son was suspected of a jewel theft in England, he left abruptly."

"I suppose so," said the President again.

"So that's how it stands at this hour, Mr. President," said Bailey. "It appears that the matter is not simple."

"What have they done with the girl?"

"The sympathy for her melted in five minutes when they found out she was suspected in the theft. It seems a very substantial amount of jewelry was taken in the burglary—at the earl's mansion south of London. The value may be as much as half a million pounds, which is —what?—more than two million dollars. Scotland Yard regarded it as an inside job all along, I understand. Anyway, Pamela's been booked on suspicion of murder, and a few minutes ago they took her off to be locked up."

"She denies everything?"

"Oh, absolutely. Stiff-upper-lip sort of young woman. She didn't cry. I understand she did when she learned Garber was dead, but she hasn't since."

"The reporters are there now, I imagine," said the President.

"I am up to my . . . backside in them, Mr. President."

"Well, we don't know anything about all this, do we, Bailey? Only what we are told."

"No, sir. Nothing."

"You are an observer, Bailey. Don't stick your nib in. If anyone asks what my position is, it is simply to want a thorough investigation and evenhanded justice. You understand? The matter has no political significance. Right?"

"That is absolutely right, Mr. President."

"Good. Don't do anything to give it any."

"We are absolutely impartial, Mr. President."

"Bailey," said the President, "I have never been so totally impartial on anything before in my whole life."

2

Eleanor Roosevelt did not slam doors. Yet there were those in the White House who would have sworn she did. The purposeful pace with which she moved from room to room *suggested* the impatient slamming of doors behind her. As she entered the White House on that sunshiny July morning, her pace was even more purposeful than usual. She had canceled a breakfast meeting in New York and had caught an early train for Washington. She carried, as she strode into the West Wing, an oversized straw purse stuffed with the *Times, The Daily News,* and the *Post.* She wore a white straw hat, a pink-flowered silk-crêpe summer dress, white gloves, and low-heeled white shoes. When she came to Grace Tully's desk outside the Oval Office, Miss Tully rose, smiled, and was about to say good morning and remark that it was a nice day when Mrs. Roosevelt cut in urgently.

"Grace, I *must* see the President immediately. Who's with him?"

Missy stepped out of her office. "Good morning," she said. "The President is with Senator George. Can I—"

"Oh, *Missy,* have you seen these *stories?*"

Missy glanced at the folded-open newspaper Mrs. Roosevelt had pulled from her purse. "I am aware of what's happened," said Missy. "The President was informed last evening."

"He should have telephoned me in New York. Indeed, Sue Brenner did call, after midnight. I changed my plans and rushed back. It is a most dreadful thing, Missy."

"Yes," said Missy. "The President was distressed to hear about it."

Mrs. Roosevelt sighed heavily, with an air of the frustration she in fact felt from having hurried all the way from New York only to be stopped short of the door to her husband's office.

Missy glanced at her watch. "Let me have some tea brought," she said. "Senator George will be out in about ten minutes, and the Greek ambassador, who is next, can be kept waiting five minutes."

"Five minutes," said Mrs. Roosevelt. "So I'm to have five minutes. Ah, well . . . Tea."

Fifteen minutes later, Missy rang the President's telephone to remind him that Senator George had overstayed his appointment and to tell him the First Lady was waiting. A minute later, Mrs. Roosevelt and the senator exchanged frosty greetings outside the open door of the Oval Office, and she went in.

The President was lighting a cigarette. "Good morning, dear Babs," he said. "How is everyone in New York?"

"Oh, Franklin!" she said. "Have you seen these horrible stories about Pamela Rush-Hodgeborne?"

"I know about the problem," said the President.

"I understand the poor child is in *jail*. It is outrageous."

The President sighed. "Well," he said carefully, "the evidence against her is . . . considerable. Bailey of Secret Service spent the evening at police headquarters and phoned me twice. That the girl is a suspect in a burglary in England doesn't help."

"Franklin," said Mrs. Roosevelt firmly. "You can't believe that Pamela Rush-Hodgeborne is guilty of a jewel theft, much less of murder. You must at least get her out of jail."

The President shook his head. "I cannot interfere," he said.

"Cannot?" asked Mrs. Roosevelt archly. "Or will not?"

"People who are charged with murder are held in jail, Babs. I can't order the D.C. police to release her just because she is employed by you and you believe her innocent. I did what I could last night. I sent along through Bailey a request that the investigation be thorough and that evenhanded justice be administered."

"Oh, *dear*," said Mrs. Roosevelt. She clicked her tongue and shook her head. "Does 'evenhanded justice' mean that poor little girl has to be confined in some noisome jail cell until she is proved innocent?"

The President tapped his holdered cigarette on the edge of an ashtray. "Babs," he said. "Maybe the girl is not innocent."

"She *is* innocent, Franklin," said Mrs. Roosevelt. "I know she is."

"You must not interfere," the President said with emphasis. "The people involved in the investigation know our interest and will do a good job. If you stick your nib in, dear Babs, it will just generate more publicity, and that can only do the girl harm."

"I am *going* to look into the matter, Franklin. I will be circumspect, but I could not live with myself if I did not do all I could to help Pamela. After all, she is in some sense my responsibility. It was at my instance that she stayed in the United States and came to Washington."

"I cannot dissuade you?"

Mrs. Roosevelt shook her head primly. "It is an obligation."

Before she left the White House to keep her appointment with the chief of detectives, District of Columbia Police, Mrs. Roosevelt sent a wire:

> REBECCA, COUNTESS OF CRITTENDEN
> AUSTIN HOUSE
> BASINGSTOKE, HAMPS
>
> DEAR PAMELA ARRESTED, CHARGED WITH MURDER OF
> PHILIP GARBER STOP AM MOST DISTRESSED, DOING ALL
> POSSIBLE TO CLARIFY MATTER, PROVE HER INNOCENCE
> STOP SEND ALL DETAILS OF HER, GARBER'S EMPLOY STOP
> SHE, GARBER SUSPECTS IN BURGLARY IN YOUR HOME STOP
> SEND DETAILS BURGLARY STOP
>
> ELEANOR ROOSEVELT
> WHITE HOUSE

Edward Kennelly, chief of detectives, received Mrs. Roosevelt as Bailey had arranged it—at an obscure side door—and escorted her through the halls to his office.

"Well, it is an unfortunate matter, ma'am," he said. He was a tall, red-faced, white-haired Irishman and spoke with a brogue. "It is highly irregular for me to give you any information beyond what has been released to the press. But, of course, seein' who you are, I will give you every cooperation."

"I would appreciate that." Kennelly had no doubt been warned that the First Lady was convinced of the innocence of Pamela Rush-

Hodgeborne and was outraged by her arrest; and Mrs. Roosevelt had been at pains to disarm him with a ready smile and soft voice. "It is just, you know, that the girl is so—so *innocent.*"

"She is a lady. I will say that for her," said Kennelly.

"Yet you are convinced she is guilty of murder. I wonder if you could tell me what evidence you have that impels you to think so?"

"Well, that's what's irregular—I mean, tellin' you the details. But, as I say, seein' as who you are . . ."

"I am not insensitive to the awkwardness of your position, Captain Kennelly," said Mrs. Roosevelt. "You may perhaps understand that my own is awkward, too. Pamela was in some sense a guest of mine, in another sense almost a daughter, since I hired her and kept her in America when she would have gone home to England."

"Yes. Well, ma'am," said Kennelly with a sigh, "uh, the short of it is that we received a call about a quarter to eight last evening. It was from a Dr. Mills. He had been called to Miss Rush-Hodgeborne's apartment—called, I might say, by Miss Rush-Hodgeborne, who had telephoned and asked him to come in a hurry. She said that Mr. Garber had collapsed and seemed to be very ill. The doctor went to her apartment, examined Mr. Garber, and immediately recognized the symptoms of cyanide poisoning. I mean, Garber smelled like bitter almonds and all that, you know. The department sent a car on the hurry-up, and when the officers arrived, Garber was already dead."

"Cyanide?" asked Mrs. Roosevelt.

"It's a terrible poison," said Kennelly solemnly. "If a person gets any considerable dose of it, he dies almost instantly. It's really a terrible poison."

"Go on, please."

Kennelly nodded. "Detectives arrived. It didn't take them long to find out how the cyanide got into Garber. The smell of the stuff was in a glass he had been drinking from. He'd begun to drink an Old Fashioned cocktail. You know, it's made with sugar and bitters and whiskey, with maybe a maraschino cherry in it. This one had a maraschino cherry in it. What was left in that glass has been to the lab, ma'am. It had enough potassium cyanide in it to have killed half a dozen men."

"How could he have drunk something that smelled of deadly poison?" asked Mrs. Roosevelt.

"Well, ma'am, the smell is not wholly unpleasant. We think the odor of the poison mingled with the smell of the bitters enough to disguise it. It probably tasted odd, all right, but he swallowed a little of it, and that was enough. It only takes a little."

"So you think she put it in his drink?"

"She mixed the cocktail, ma'am. She admits that. The poison was in the bitters. We brought the bottle to the lab, too. The bitters were laced with potassium cyanide."

Mrs. Roosevelt smiled and shook her head. "I don't think it makes much sense, Captain Kennelly," she said. "If she wanted to murder Philip Garber, why would she poison him in her own apartment, call a doctor for him, and leave the glass and bottle with the poison in them for the police to find? Why didn't she rinse out his glass, maybe even mix another drink, without poison, for the police to find? Why didn't she pour out the poisoned bitters, too? Anyway, how would a twenty-one-year-old English girl come into possession of so deadly a substance?"

"Those were my thoughts as well, ma'am—last night. But then some more facts came to our attention, and—"

"You mean about the jewel theft at Austin House?"

"Yes, ma'am. Scotland Yard lists Philip Garber and Pamela Rush-Hodgeborne as principal suspects in that crime. I suppose you know, ma'am, that more than two million dollars' worth of gems were taken in that burglary."

"The Earl and Countess of Crittenden certainly never regarded her as a suspect."

"I have to wonder, ma'am, how much they knew about the young woman who was their children's tutor. I wonder if they knew—and, excuse me, I want to put this delicately—that there was what we might call a meretricious relationship between Mr. Garber and Miss Rush-Hodgeborne. I'm afraid I must ask if you yourself, ma'am, knew that a female member of your staff entertained a young man overnight in her apartment at least twice a week."

Mrs. Roosevelt blushed lightly. "It doesn't suggest she's guilty of murder."

"She admits that she and Garber had an intimate relationship—

nd, indeed, had one while they were living in the earl's household. I
vish, however, she would be as frank about the burglary. On that
ubject, she is distinctly not forthcoming."

"Maybe she knows nothing about it," suggested Mrs. Roosevelt.

"Yes, ma'am. Maybe. But allow me to show you something."

The chief of detectives opened the drawer of his desk and removed
a large white envelope, from which he gingerly took a round gold
ocket watch. Attached by one heavy gold link to a gold bar with a
teel pin on the back, the watch was designed to be worn on a
voman's lapel. Indeed, as Mrs. Roosevelt looked at it, she reflected
hat it was very much like one she wore herself, in colder weather
vhen she wore a jacket. The chief difference was that this one was
arger than most watches of its kind.

"Notice," said Kennelly. He unscrewed the back of the watch and
ifted it off. Immediately she could see that the works were distinctly
maller than the face. The size of the works left room inside the
vatch for a circular tube slightly more than a quarter of an inch in
diameter. The tube did not complete the circle by about half an inch,
nd its ends were plugged with small wads of white cotton, which
Kennelly now plucked out.

"What do you suppose you could hide in there, ma'am?" he asked.

"You are suggesting a diamond, I suppose?"

"About two dozen good-sized diamonds, I should estimate," said
Kennelly. "And, in fact . . ."

From the white envelope he took a small glassine envelope. It was
ealed shut, but through the transparent glassine she could see a
diamond.

"She denies she knew her watch had a hidey-hole in it," said
Kennelly. "She denies ever having seen the diamond before. But I
am compelled to ask, Mrs. Roosevelt, if the girl is innocent, why was
he carrying in a hiding place in her watch a diamond that has been
appraised as worth maybe six thousand dollars? And how many more
were in there at one time?"

"How many, indeed, were stolen in the first place?"

"A great many more than the two dozen or so that could fit into
his watch," said Kennelly, replacing watch and glassine envelope in
he white envelope and putting it in his desk. "As I said, maybe two
million dollars' worth of diamonds, emeralds, sapphires, and so on."

He locked his desk drawer. "An expert is to examine this diamond, to see if it can be matched to the inventory."

"I still cannot imagine where Pamela would get potassium cyanide."

"It is not an uncommon chemical, unfortunately," said the detective. "It doesn't often turn up in criminal investigations in this country, but it might, since it's easy enough to obtain. It is used in a number of industrial processes, including the refining of gold and silver from ores. It can be bought from laboratory supply houses. Of course, if you were a member of a gang of criminals engaged in stealing diamonds—"

"No," said Mrs. Roosevelt firmly. "Pamela is *not* a member of a criminal gang."

"I'm sorry, ma'am," said Kennelly. "I could regain my sympathy for her if she would tell us why her watch has a secret compartment in it and why we found a valuable diamond in there. She must know something about that."

"Perhaps she would tell me," said Mrs. Roosevelt. "I would like to see the girl."

The detective glanced at his wristwatch. "Could you give us an hour, ma'am? The girl is being questioned by F.B.I. agents at the moment."

"The third degree?"

Kennelly smiled. "No, ma'am. Nothing like that. But you know Edgar Hoover. If there's a crime with the potential for public attention, he's going to stick his nose in and take as much of the credit as possible."

"I do indeed know Mr. Hoover," said Mrs. Roosevelt distastefully. "You can turn over rocks in the woods and find his like anytime." She sighed. "I have an appointment I must keep in an hour. I will return after that."

"We'll make the girl available to you, Mrs. Roosevelt."

Her appointment was at the British Embassy. Her visit was unofficial and confidential, and she was received not by Lord Lothian, the ambassador, but by Sir Rodney Harcourt, second secretary, the legal officer of the embassy. It being teatime, Harcourt sat down with her in a small library, where tea and sandwiches and small pastries were served on a silver tray. Harcourt was a man of sixty years, white-haired but erect with almost military rigidity; he was dressed in a gray-striped black suit with vest, a wing collar, and bow tie. His watch chain hung across his vest. His white handkerchief was loosely folded into a tall peak and rose half the width of his lapel.

"Ah, Mrs. Rose-vult," he said. "It is good to see you. I could only wish the occasion of your visit were a happier one."

Mrs. Roosevelt sipped her tea. "I do hope, Sir Rodney, that your government will do all it can to defend this poor English girl and secure her release."

"We have every confidence in American justice," said Sir Rodney smoothly.

"As have I, Sir Rodney—when the courts have before them all the pertinent facts. It seems to me that your government could be of much help to Pamela Rush-Hodgeborne by gathering information and seeing to it that it reaches our investigators. I am thinking in particular of this ludicrous suggestion that the girl may have had something to do with the theft of jewels from Austin House."

A frown passed over the face of the second secretary. "Yes," he said. "The difficulty seems to be, Mrs. Rose-vult, that Miss Rush-Hodgeborne may in fact have been an accomplice to the burglars. The evidence does suggest so."

"What evidence is that, Sir Rodney?"

"As you know, Miss Rush-Hodgeborne—as indeed was Mr. Philip Garber, the murder victim—was employed by the Earl of Crittenden in his house at the time of the burglary. The circumstances of the crime persuasively argue that there was inside participation, as they say. Miss Rush-Hodgeborne and Mr. Garber were among the very few members of the household staff who had access to the earl's library on a daily basis and probably knew where his safe was concealed."

"Speculation," said Mrs. Roosevelt.

"More than that, unfortunately," said Sir Rodney. "There is another circumstance that argues against Miss Rush-Hodgeborne."

"You mean that they found a diamond in her watch?"

"Did they indeed? I hadn't heard *that.*"

Mrs. Roosevelt fluttered a hand. "Yes. Well. They found one diamond in her watch. But what is the circumstance you were about to mention?"

Sir Rodney sighed. He put down his teacup and clasped his hands before his chin. "You must understand," he said, "that the theft of the gems from Austin House was no ordinary jewel theft. In fact, none of the stolen gems were in the form of jewelry. They were unset stones, all of them. The earl is a collector and to some extent a dealer in fine gems. He owns, for example, the famous Alexandra emerald that once belonged to the Czarina of Russia. The emerald, incidentally, was not taken. It was on loan at the time, to the British Museum. Many of the stolen gems were, however, known and identifiable by an expert."

"How can anyone tell one diamond from another?" asked Mrs. Roosevelt. "I mean, beyond weight and so on. There must be thousands of each cut and size."

Sir Rodney shook his head. "They are known by size and weight, of course, but also by color, cut, flaws. I am not myself an initiate into the mysteries of gemology, but I understand there is a system of identification, and many stones can be positively identified." He drew a deep breath. "Four diamonds positively identified as among those stolen from the Earl of Crittenden have been found in the United States in the past few months. They were taken when a notorious New York purchaser of stolen property—a fence, I believe is the term—was arrested in May. Their total value exceeded five thousand pounds."

"Have others been found?"

"Yes. A few others have been recovered in England. I need hardly point out, however, that what I have just told you argues rather strongly that either Miss Rush-Hodgeborne or Mr. Garber, or both, were involved in the burglary. If the stone found in Miss Rush-Hodgeborne's watch turns out also to have been one of those stolen from Austin House, then it would seem that Miss Rush-Hodgeborne is clearly one of the thieves."

"I am not sure it would prove that, Sir Rodney," said Mrs. Roosevelt.

"Well. That is arguable, of course. In any event, when several of the stolen gems appeared in the United States in May, Scotland Yard moved Miss Rush-Hodgeborne and Mr. Garber to the top of their list of suspects. I am not sure what is proved by the fact that one of those principal suspects is now dead and that the other seems to have poisoned him—but I am sure conclusions will be drawn."

Mrs. Roosevelt nodded. "Unfortunately, they will. They will indeed. Poor Pamela!"

Sir Rodney sighed. "Yes. I understand she is a young lady of good family."

"Unhappily, Sir Rodney, Philip Garber was *not*. I speak in confidence, but his background is actually *suggestive* of a criminal nature."

"I understood his father is a congressman," protested Sir Rodney.

"Yes. But tell me, Sir Rodney, is membership in the House of Commons an absolute warranty of good character?"

The second secretary smiled. "I'm afraid it isn't," he said.

"And neither is membership in the United States Congress," said Mrs. Roosevelt. "Congressman Garber is what we in this country call a political boss. He has a most *unsavory* reputation—mostly deserved, I am afraid. Larceny may well be in the blood."

"Distressing," remarked Sir Rodney.

"Therefore, if I may I would like to suggest—no, I would like to *request*—that Scotland Yard pursue most vigorously its investigation into Philip Garber's activities during his stay in England. Poor Pamela may be that young man's innocent victim."

Sir Rodney nodded gravely. "I will communicate your request, Mrs. Rose-vult."

"In confidence, of course," she added.

"Yes. In confidence, of course."

3

"Oh, Mrs. Roosevelt," said Pamela Rush-Hodgeborne, sighing weakly. "How very nice of you. How very thoughtful."

On the other side of a heavy wire mesh, the girl sat down on a stool, leaned forward, and rested her arms on a scarred wooden shelf. She was dressed in the uniform of the District jail: a gray cotton dress with short sleeves and a square yoke. She was the very picture of a pretty young Englishwoman—faultless pale complexion with pink cheeks, big blue eyes, small upturned nose, dimpled chin, and blond hair that she wore short and natural.

"Pamela," said Mrs. Roosevelt, "I am sure you are innocent. I am absolutely certain of it."

"I am, Mrs. Roosevelt. I am," affirmed Pamela. "Though you may be the only person in the world who thinks so."

"Well, there is at least one other person who knows you are innocent," said Mrs. Roosevelt.

"Really? Who?"

"The person who killed Philip Garber."

Pamela nodded. "Yes. Oh, yes."

The policeman who had escorted Mrs. Roosevelt to the visiting room of the jail—after hours, when no one else could be there—had carried in a small, leather-covered chair from one of the offices; and she sat comfortably in the ugly, concrete-and-steel room, looking up into the face of Pamela Rush-Hodgeborne, whose stool was a little higher than the chair.

Pamela hooked one finger in the steel mesh that separated her from the First Lady. "They, uh—mean to hang me, don't they?" she asked quietly. "Or . . . in the States they electrocute people, isn't that right? They mean to do that to me, don't they?"

"Only if you're guilty," said Mrs. Roosevelt. "And that is far from proven."

"I'm afraid it *is* proven," said Pamela. "Philip died in *my* flat, of poison in a drink *I* mixed for him, and more of that poison was found in a bottle in my kitchen cabinet. Besides, they found a stolen diamond·in my watch. Oh, Mrs. Roosevelt, I am in very great trouble!"

"*I* believe you are innocent," said Mrs. Roosevelt firmly, "and I mean to do everything I can to prove it."

"I'm of course grateful," said Pamela despondently, "but I'm afraid it's all settled. The evidence is all against me."

"All that's been found," said Mrs. Roosevelt. "The proof of your innocence remains to be found. And since you *are* innocent, that proof has to be somewhere waiting to be discovered."

"But even I don't know what that proof is," said Pamela. "And"— she glanced around her—"I am a prisoner now and can't do anything to look for it."

"*I* shall look for it," said Mrs. Roosevelt.

"You? But—"

"I have some little influence. I shall have help."

Pamela blinked back a tear and wiped the corner of her eye with a finger. "Does the President believe I'm innocent?" she asked.

"Of course he does."

"Then . . . ?"

"We shall find the evidence before we ask him to do anything. And, of course, when we have the evidence, he won't have to act."

Pamela frowned and nodded. "You give me some hope, Mrs. Roosevelt. I have none except in you."

"*Well,*" said Mrs. Roosevelt, plunging a hand into her big straw bag and pulling out a small notepad with pencil attached. "We have work to do, Pamela. You must tell me everything. Everything, you understand, even if it seems to be against you."

Pamela nodded again. She leaned closer to Mrs. Roosevelt, so close that her face almost touched the wire mesh between them. "Where shall we begin?"

Pamela Rush-Hodgeborne, as she told Mrs. Roosevelt, was the daughter of an impecunious Kent schoolmaster. She was one of five children. Her father taught French to the sons of well-to-do parents, and from her earliest years Pamela had heard French as well as English spoken in her family home. It was her parents' pride that all their children should be bilingual and should have fine English-upper-class manners. That would be their inheritance, she often heard them say.

By chance, one of her father's former students was a nephew of the Earl of Crittenden, and when the nephew heard that the earl and the countess were looking for a tutor for their two small daughters, he suggested that they consider the modest and charming daughter of William Rush-Hodgeborne. So it was that in 1936 Pamela, then just eighteen years old, became a member of the earl's household.

"It was a fine opportunity for me, Mrs. Roosevelt. If it hadn't come, I would probably have married in the village and would never have seen France or . . ."

"Or America, which has turned out not to be so fine an opportunity," said Mrs. Roosevelt.

"Or America," Pamela agreed miserably.

"Tell me about Philip Garber."

Pamela swallowed. "Philip. I met him before the earl did, actually. The family was living in the townhouse on Berkeley Square, and on my days off I would often sit in the sunshine in the park or perhaps see a matinée at the cinema. Also, I visited the National Gallery and the British Museum—and all of that, you know. One day I was sitting in a chair in Hyde Park, reading and watching people rowing on the Serpentine, and a young man walking by me happened to drop his paper of chips, actually right on my feet. He was most embarrassed and apologetic, and he spoke very strangely, I thought. He was an American, one of the first I ever met. He was, of course, Philip. He was supposed to be studying at Oxford, but he had not done well in his studies, so he was in London, enjoying the town, as you might say. We became acquainted. He began to call at the house to see me. The earl is very democratic, as you may know, and he seemed glad to talk with Philip. He learned that he was the son of a congressman, and they talked at some length about America. I was always somewhat embarrassed that a young man coming to see me took so much of the earl's time. For myself, I should never have dared engage the earl in lengthy conversation."

"So how did the earl come to employ him?"

"I don't know. I believe it was at Philip's suggestion. They talked about books of account and budgets and controlling expenditures, things like that, and one day Philip said to me, 'Guess what, the earl's hired me to help straighten out his household accounts.' "

"So he moved in?"

"Well, not in London. But when we moved back to Austin House, Philip came to live there."

"And you and Philip became—how shall we say?—very good friends indeed," said Mrs. Roosevelt.

Pamela blushed and closed her eyes. "Yes," she said quietly.

"Did the earl and the countess know that?"

Pamela rested the palm of her hand on the wire mesh, letting her fingers slip through. "I don't know how much they understood," she whispered.

"Did you plan to marry Philip?"

"Well . . . we spoke of it as a possibility but one that was deferred. He said he was not yet established in life. I'm not quite sure what that meant."

Mrs. Roosevelt had as yet written nothing on her little pad. She tapped it with her pencil. "The watch, Pamela," she said. "Where did you get the watch?"

Pamela's eyes widened as if a thought had come to her. "It was a gift from Philip," she said softly.

"Have you any idea how it came to have a valuable diamond concealed inside it?"

"Not the slightest. Philip told me he bought it from a watchmaker in London. It is an antique case with modern works in it. I can only think the diamond was in it all along."

"When did he give it to you?"

"For Christmas last year."

"Before the burglary, then?"

"Oh, yes."

"Was it ever out of your possession after he gave it to you, Pamela? Did he, for example, ever return it to the watchmaker for repair or anything like that?"

Pamela shook her head, and her eyes filled with tears. "No. I cherished it, and it has never been out of my possession since the day I received it. You may have noticed that I wore it every day."

"Where did you keep it at night?"

"On my dressing table. I have no jewels. I haven't a jewel box."

"Tell me about the burglary, Pamela."

Pamela sighed. "That was a horrible experience. I woke one morning to find the whole household in a monstrous uproar. The house had been broken into in the night. The earl's safe was open, and all his precious stones were gone. Two of the earl's dogs—which would have been prowling the grounds—were dead. The alarm system had failed. By the time I dressed and came down, the house was full of constables. Shortly, men from Scotland Yard arrived. Everyone was suspected. I was questioned at great length. Very severely, too. So was Philip. They searched our rooms and our persons. I mean, Mrs. Roosevelt, they brought in a *woman* to search me—if you know what I mean. And the questions were most embarrassing."

"How is that?"

"Well . . . They required each of the household staff to account for all the hours of the night. Where were we? Did we arise in the night for any reason? Did we see or hear anything? On and on. Philip had to admit that he had—that I had . . ." She hung her head. "Oh, Mrs. Roosevelt," she whispered, *"he had spent the night in my room!"*

"We needn't talk about that," said Mrs. Roosevelt quickly. "If he was with you all night, then he could not have done anything to help the burglars. Is that not right?"

"Yes."

Mrs. Roosevelt turned down the corners of her mouth, and for a moment she frowned and considered. "Er . . . he could not have left your room in the night, while you were asleep?"

Pamela shook her head. "I don't think so," she said very quietly.

Mrs. Roosevelt sighed, then stiffened. "Much may turn on it, Pamela," she said. "Did you tell the detectives he could not have left your room in the night without your knowing it?"

Pamela nodded. "That is what I told them."

"Was it true?"

Pamela shook her head violently. "Mrs. Roosevelt," she sobbed. "You are compelling me to tell you *he was in my bed with me!*"

"My dear," said Mrs. Roosevelt soothingly, "in years past, when my husband and I slept in the same bed, he sometimes got up in the night, to visit the bathroom and so on, and I did not always know it. Had you anything to drink before you went to bed that night?"

"Yes. Some cognac. Philip brought a bottle of cognac to my room."

Mrs. Roosevelt made a note. "The earl's cognac?"

"Yes. I was not pleased that Philip had brought it, but he said the earl had told him he could drink from the cellar as he wished. He never took much advantage of that privilege, actually."

"Because Philip favored an American drink—an Old Fashioned cocktail, is that not right?"

Pamela sighed. "Yes. He would hardly take any other kind of spirits, even excellent brandy. In England it was not easy to obtain the American whiskey—bourbon— that he insisted he must have to mix it properly, and he went to great pains to get it. He would not drink an Old Fashioned mixed with Scotch. He must have his mulled sugar and his bitters and his bourbon. I learned to mix them for him. That is, of course, what I mixed for him last evening."

"Returning to the burglary," said Mrs. Roosevelt. "You say they searched both of you very thoroughly."

"Quite thoroughly."

"They searched the house and grounds, of course."

"Quite thoroughly."

"You and Philip were more suspected than others in the house, isn't that right?"

"Yes. Because we were not exactly servants. We never had to explain why we were anywhere in the house. Our status in the household allowed us access to the earl's library at any time. I did in fact know where his safe was. The earl had shown me his gems. He had shown them to Philip as well. The detectives believed the rest of the household staff were ignorant of the safe. Also, I think the detectives decided Philip and I were not very honorable people when they learned he had spent the night in my room."

"How was the safe opened, Pamela?"

"Expertly. It was not blown open with explosives, or drilled, or anything like that. Whoever opened it simply opened it. At first the detectives believed that it had been unlocked by someone who had learned the combination. But the earl insisted he had never told anyone the combination and had never written it down. I later heard that because it was an old safe, an expert safecracker could open it by feeling the vibrations as the dial was turned or by listening to the tumblers."

"So far as Scotland Yard was concerned, you were a suspect. But the earl and the countess did not suspect you, did they?"

"They protested vehemently when the detectives laid suspicion on me."

"And Philip?"

Pamela sighed. "The detectives told the earl that Philip spent the night in my room and that I said he had not left my side all night. So far as the earl was concerned, my word cleared Philip."

"When the countess brought you to this country and recommended you to me, she knew about you and Philip?"

"I suppose so. She never spoke of it."

Mrs. Roosevelt put her notepad back in her purse. "Pamela," she said. "Were you and Philip in love?"

"No," said Pamela.

"Still, you had resumed your former relationship with him, had you not?"

Pamela nodded. "I was lonely, Mrs. Roosevelt. He *was* an engaging fellow, you know. He was a friend."

Mrs. Roosevelt pursed her lips for a moment. "I suppose the standards of your generation and those of mine are rather dramatically different."

Pamela hung her head. "I am sorry. I'm afraid I have betrayed your trust."

"Not at all!" exclaimed Mrs. Roosevelt. "Your standards and those of my children are not dissimilar. I am interested in changing the world, but not in this respect. Tell me, though, Pamela, do you think Philip was pursuing you when he came to Washington and sought a job at the White House?"

"He talked that way at first. I didn't believe him, though."

"Ah. You didn't believe him. Why not?"

"He was engaging, amusing . . . loving. But he was a rather slippery fellow, don't you think?"

"I didn't know him, Pamela."

Pamela ran one hand down the wire mesh. "Even before the burglary, I had decided I could never marry Philip. I felt that if ever I had been in love with him, it had been an error. He was superficial, Mrs. Roosevelt. He was insincere."

"What do you know of his life in England? I mean, what do you know of his life other than at Austin House?"

"He had friends," Pamela said. "From time to time he would go up to London and spend a day or so with them. He was mysterious as to who they were."

"Do you have any idea who they were?"

"No."

"What were his interests? He was in England to study but didn't. What had he been doing when you met him in London?"

"He was interested in what I think you would call high living. He liked to gamble—to play at cards. He tried to teach me to play a card game. Poker, I believe it was called. Yes, poker. He was also interested in horse racing. He had no interest in the country, none in art or music or literature. He spoke no language but American English. I should say of him, to do him justice, that he was a genius at mathematics. The earl was very grateful to him for his expert work on the estate accounts. The earl told me that Philip had saved him two thousand pounds a year in duplicated or unnecessary expenditures."

Mrs. Roosevelt nodded. "All right, Pamela. Tell me about last night."

Once more, Pamela ran a hand down the heavy wire mesh that imprisoned her. "I worked in your office until five-thirty. Philip came up from the usher's office about that time. We walked to my flat. It was a pleasant evening, though quite warm, and we walked that distance. I should say that he came for a drink almost every evening. He himself brought the bourbon—which I kept in my kitchen—and the cognac. Two or three nights a week we had dinner together, sometimes in my flat, sometimes out. If we had dinner, then usually he stayed the night. He came for a drink last night, and we hadn't said whether we would eat together and . . . You understand."

"Quite."

Pamela ran her hand across her mouth. "We arrived about six, a little after. We listened to a news broadcast—and heard, incidentally, that you were in New York. Philip was quite casual, as he usually was. He took off his jacket and necktie. After we heard the news, he asked me to mix him a cocktail. I went in the kitchen and prepared it as usual. He was quite particular about how it should be mixed, and I had learned to do it to his taste. I had a bit of whiskey myself as I mixed his Old Fashioned."

"Did you yourself ever drink Old Fashioneds?" asked Mrs. Roosevelt.

"No. I tried them a few times but didn't care for them. They require ice, which makes them quite cold. Odd drinks, I always thought."

"Go on."

"I mixed his cocktail as always. I poured myself a bit more whiskey and carried the glasses into the living room. Philip took his. He sniffed at it, as though it had an unusual odor. Then he drank a swallow of it. 'What'd you put in this?' he asked. He turned up his nose over it, but he drank another swallow. Then, very suddenly, and without another word, he gasped, doubled over, and collapsed out of his chair and onto the floor. By the time I got to him, he was in some sort of convulsions, writhing, whipping about. I went to the telephone and called Dr. Mills, who lives in another flat in the building. By the time I put down the telephone, Philip was no longer moving."

"Pamela, where did you obtain the bottle of bitters?"

"Philip brought it himself. It was half empty. I had mixed him drinks out of it many times before."

"The bourbon?"

"A half-empty bottle. He'd drunk from it the night before."

"Who was in your apartment between that night and last night?"

"Only Philip and I."

Mrs. Roosevelt took a deep breath. "Pamela," she said. "What explanation do you have for the fact that the police found a large quantity of potassium cyanide in the bitters, as well as in the glass from which Philip had been drinking?"

"Explanation?" Pamela asked. "Indeed, ma'am, I have none."

When Mrs. Roosevelt returned to the White House, a wire from the Countess of Crittenden was waiting for her.

MRS. ELEANOR ROOSEVELT
THE WHITE HOUSE
WASHINGTON, D.C., U.S.A.

IMPOSSIBLE REPEAT IMPOSSIBLE PAMELA RUSH-HODGE-BORNE COULD BE GUILTY OF MURDER OR BURGLARY STOP THE EARL WILL CALL ON FOREIGN OFFICE, SCOTLAND YARD TOMORROW TO DEMAND FULL COOPERATION IN ESTABLISHING HER INNOCENCE STOP DETAILS FOLLOW STOP GIVE PAMELA ASSURANCE OUR SYMPATHY AND SUPPORT STOP

REBECCA

Mrs. Roosevelt wired back:

REBECCA, COUNTESS OF CRITTENDEN
AUSTIN HOUSE
BASINGSTOKE, HAMPS

ASK EARL TO WIRE MAKE AND MODEL OF SAFE OPENED BY BURGLARS STOP ALSO ASK HIM TO INQUIRE OF SCOTLAND YARD IF BOTTLE COGNAC WAS FOUND IN PAMELA'S ROOM MORNING AFTER BURGLARY STOP

ELEANOR

Hurrying into the west hall about seven, on her way to her room and, as she hoped, to a relaxing bath, Mrs. Roosevelt was surprised to find the hall vacant. The President was not there mixing cocktails. Missy was not there. No one. She knocked on the door of the President's bedroom, then entered. Arthur was with the President, helping him with his white dinner jacket.

"Not dressed?" asked the President.

"Franklin, you know I am very well organized and punctual about appointments," she said. "It has been a trying day, though. What have I overlooked?"

"Nothing important." He laughed. "Only a little informal dinner arranged by Secretary Hull. You have ten minutes, my dear."

"Is it here?" she asked.

"No, thank God. I get to go out to dinner tonight."

"With whom, Franklin?" she asked, a little irritated.

"Secretary Hull, Henry Stimson, Sol Bloom, Senator Vandenberg, and a few others. It's at the Dutch Embassy. It's been on your calendar, Babs. Where've you been so late?"

"At the *jail*, Franklin."

"See anyone we know?" asked the President.

"Only poor Pamela."

"Ah. Well, please eschew that subject during the dinner. The topic for conversation tonight is, I imagine, the defense of Europe against Herr Hitler."

She took some pride in her flexibility, in her ability to rise to an occasion, and by seven-thirty, when the car brought them to the door of the embassy of the Netherlands and they were greeted at the door by the ambassador and his wife, Mrs. Roosevelt was dressed in a light green silk summer gown and was able to smile graciously and with enthusiasm, as if she had spent the afternoon preparing for the evening.

At dinner she was seated between the Dutch ambassador and Senator Arthur Vandenberg, the Republican from Michigan, a one-time isolationist slowly turning internationalist.

"We hear, Mr. President," said the ambassador, "that the German government is making approaches to the government of the Soviet

Union, looking perhaps for a relaxation of tensions in Eastern Europe. Can you confirm or deny that?"

The President was enjoying the meal and the evening. Between courses, he was leaning back comfortably, his cigarette holder atilt, his smile broad. "I seem to be one of the last people to receive word from Hitler and Stalin, Mr. Ambassador," he said. "Somehow they are a bit reticent with me."

"Should we regard it as good news if it is true?" the ambassador asked.

"Relaxation of tensions anywhere may be regarded as good news," said Senator Vandenberg.

Henry Stimson shook his head gravely. "I think it better for the peace of Europe and for the welfare of democratic nations in Western Europe for those two scoundrels to remain at each other's throats," he said. "If Hitler can protect his back by making some kind of agreement with Stalin, it will free him to make more demands and even to risk war in the west."

This statement for a long moment subdued all conversation around the table, and when talk resumed it was fragmented and lighter.

Senator Vandenberg leaned closer to Mrs. Roosevelt. "Do you think Henry is right?" he asked.

"I'm afraid so," she said.

The senator lifted his dark, bushy eyebrows and shook his head. "I am sorry to read about the problem with your English secretary," he said.

"She is quite innocent," said Mrs. Roosevelt confidently.

"I hope so," he replied.

Mrs. Roosevelt cocked her head and looked quizzically at Senator Vandenberg for a moment. Then she said, "Tell me, Senator, do you know anything at all about cracking safes?"

The senator laughed. "I'm afraid it's not in my line," he said.

The Dutch ambassador, who had overheard, turned toward her. "Do you refer to the illegal opening of strongboxes and strong rooms?" he asked.

"Yes," said Mrs. Roosevelt, with a small smile.

"I have some knowledge of such matters," said the ambassador. "Many years ago I was trained as an intelligence officer, and I learned something of the techniques of opening locked steel doors."

"How fascinating," said Mrs. Roosevelt. "Do you mind if I ask you a question about it?"

"Not at all."

She glanced across the table at the President, who was regarding her with amused curiosity. He had overheard a word or two and knew the subject of her conversation. She smiled at him.

"Well, Mr. Ambassador," she said. "An element of this distressing case against my English secretary involves the opening of what I am told was a rather old wall safe in an English country home."

"That of the Earl of Crittenden," said the ambassador.

"Yes," she said, surprised.

"What would you like to know?"

"With how much difficulty would such a safe be opened? It was not *broken* open, just opened, by someone who knew how to work the combination lock without knowing the combination."

"After dinner," said the ambassador, "with your kind permission, I will show you how to open such a strongbox. Indeed, I believe I can teach you to do it yourself, in only a few minutes."

The safe was in a second-floor office. The President's wheelchair could not readily negotiate the stairs, so he was brought up on a cramped lift, clutching a snifter of Napoleon brandy between his hands, grinning with pleasure at the adventure, while Mrs. Roosevelt —and Henry Stimson, who had professed a strong curiosity— mounted the stairs and followed the ambassador through a corridor.

The safe was mounted in the wall of a small, modestly furnished office. The maroon finish of the safe gleamed in the yellow lamplight, and small bright reflections flashed off its polished brass knob and handle. An elaborately detailed spread-winged eagle was painted in gold and black above the combination dial.

"Strongboxes like this were most common fifty years ago," said the ambassador. "I do not know the combination. It is kept by my cipher clerk. Still, I think I can open it. I hope I do not embarrass myself by proving wrong."

He pulled up a chair for Mrs. Roosevelt. Stimson pushed the President's wheelchair close. The three watched intently as the ambassador set to work.

The ambassador, wearing his white dinner jacket with decorations, enjoyed the drama of the moment. Kneeling, he put his ear close to the door of the safe and slowly turned the dial. He touched the dial only with the tips of his fingers. With his left hand he betrayed his nervousness over the possibility of failure by pinching his gray spade beard.

"It requires a certain delicacy," he said quietly. "Ah. Yes, and . . . ah. And . . . ah . . ."

He turned the dial this way and that for no more than three minutes, and then, with a grunt of triumph and satisfaction, he twisted the handle and pulled open the door.

"You see? It is old. It is also virtually worthless for securing anything valuable. Unfortunately, few people know that. Unfortunately, too, the people who would wish to open such boxes do know it."

"Marvelous," said the President. "And you say one can learn this technique very readily?"

"Indeed," said the ambassador. He slammed the door shut and twisted the dial. "Would Mrs. Roosevelt like to try?"

"Yes," she said enthusiastically. "Very much."

"Good. Please to remove your gloves."

As the ambassador had done, Mrs. Roosevelt knelt on the floor, put her ear to the door of the safe, and gingerly twisted the dial. At first she heard nothing, felt nothing. Then she felt a slight resistance against her turning, followed immediately by an abrupt release of that resistance and a faint thump inside the door. She turned the dial in the opposite direction until she felt and heard the same. On the next turn she missed the resistance and thump and so had to start again. On her second try she missed the first resistance and thump. Finally, on the fourth try, she dialed the combination and opened the safe.

"Bravo!" cried the President.

"You see?" said the ambassador. "Easy, is it not? Of course, they are not all so easy. Others require different techniques. Indeed, some need drilling, and others require explosives to open them. The newer boxes are difficult indeed. But these old ones . . ." He shrugged. "In here we keep nothing but the cipher clerk's love letters."

"It has been very instructive, Mr. Ambassador," said Mrs. Roosevelt. "It suggests to me the solution to a difficult problem that has been troubling me all day. I am grateful to you."

The next morning a wire came from the Countess of Crittenden:

MRS. ELEANOR ROOSEVELT
THE WHITE HOUSE
WASHINGTON, D.C., U.S.A.

OUR SAFE MANUFACTURED BY EMPIRE SAFE CABINET
COMPANY, MODEL G-23, DATED 1887 STOP SCOTLAND
YARD INVENTORY ITEMS IN PAMELA'S ROOM MORNING AF-
TER BURGLARY INCLUDED NO BOTTLE COGNAC STOP EX-
PECT FULL COOPERATION FOREIGN OFFICE, SCOTLAND
YARD STOP PLEASE SPARE NOTHING TO WIN PAMELA'S
VINDICATION STOP WILL FLY STATES IMMEDIATELY IF
HELPFUL STOP

REBECCA

Mrs. Roosevelt telephoned Sir Rodney Harcourt at the British Embassy. When he came on the line, she asked him if he could look
around the embassy and learn if there were any Empire Safe Cabinet
Company safes, preferably dating from the nineteenth century, on
the premises. He said he would look and ring back.

She attended a luncheon of the Women's Coalition for Agrarian
Justice. Afterward she received a delegation of Iowa members of the
American Association of University Women, who presented her a
plaque. Only after the delegation had left could she return the call
that had come from Sir Rodney.

"We do in fact," he said, "have an old strongbox here, an Empire,
built in 1891. It's in the office of the naval attaché."

"Would you permit me to examine it?" she asked.

"I am quite sure it could be arranged. When would you like to see
it?"

"Now, please. I will drive over immediately, if it's convenient."

"Uh . . . Well, yes, of course."

Her visit was again unofficial and meant to go unnoticed. She
hurried into the embassy, was met by Sir Rodney Harcourt, and
introduced by him to Captain Giles Padwick, the naval attaché.

In his office, the attaché showed her the Empire safe. It was concealed behind a hidden door in the oak paneling. With no flamboyant eagle painted on its plain black surface, with heavy gray steel dial and handle, the safe looked solid and strong. Its formidable appearance was in discouraging contrast to the handsome model she had been taught to open at the Dutch Embassy.

"Well," she said, with an ingenuous smile at Sir Rodney and Captain Padwick. "Do you mind if I examine it more closely?"

"Of course not, ma'am," said the tall, ruddy naval officer. "Examine it as you wish."

"Thank you," said Mrs. Roosevelt.

She removed her white gloves and put them in her purse. She took off her white straw hat and laid it aside on a desk. Then she knelt before the safe, tested the dial, and put her ear to the door. As Sir Rodney and the captain gaped with astonishment, she began to turn the dial, feeling the pressure, listening for the faint thump of a tumbler in the big old lock. This lock was more subtle than the one at the Dutch Embassy. It was only after she had twisted the dial clockwise four times that she detected the feeble resistance of polished metal against polished metal, felt the dial pass that point of resistance, and heard a metallic thump deep inside the heavy steel door.

She looked up and smiled at the two Englishmen. "It is a very interesting lock," she said.

She turned the dial in the opposite direction, slowly, with the sensitive tips of her fingers, pressing her ear to the door. This time she did not feel the resistance, but she believed she heard the thump of a tumbler, and she accepted that. She turned in the other direction. The working of this tumbler was more pronounced, and she was confident of what she felt. She turned the dial again. Again the resistance was almost imperceptible, and the thump faint.

She paused. She tried the handle. It would not turn. The safe remained locked. She frowned. She must start over. She glanced up at the two men, who were probably certain by now that the wife of the President of the United States was as dotty as Queen Victoria. She smiled at them and put her fingers again on the dial.

Suddenly, a thought! Maybe the combination had five numbers, or six, not just four. She eased the dial around again, feeling and listening, and—sure enough!—she felt a tumbler fall. She tried the handle again and . . . It turned! She tugged, and the door swung back.

She turned her face quickly away from the exposed interior of the safe. "Oh, I'm sorry," she said quickly. "I hope there's nothing secret in there."

She shared tea with Sir Rodney Harcourt for the second time in two days.

"I have two bits of news for you," he said when their tea was poured and she sat quietly munching a cucumber sandwich. "One rather bad, I'm afraid."

"That the safe opened so easily was good news," she said. "Perhaps I can endure an item of bad news."

"A jeweler from New York this morning examined the stone found in Pamela Rush-Hodgeborne's lapel watch," said Sir Rodney. "It is indeed a diamond stolen from the Earl of Crittenden at the time of the Austin House burglary."

Mrs. Roosevelt shrugged. "I should have been surprised if it weren't," she said. "I am amazed, however, at the value of the collection."

"Yes. Well . . . the earl inherited the holdings of his grandfather, you understand—"

"The fourth earl," Mrs. Roosevelt said, nodding.

"Yes. And the fourth Earl of Crittenden returned from India in 1893 with an immense fortune in gems. When he died, the part of those gems that remained at Austin House was appraised at more than a quarter of a million pounds. The present earl has traded, buying diamonds, selling others. . . . His loss may be as much as half a million pounds."

"Insured?"

"For the most part. Some part of the collection was not listed on the inventory. Even so, the insurance companies have already paid him more than two hundred thousand pounds, and they expect to pay a great deal more."

"I am glad to hear the earl and the countess are not impoverished," said Mrs. Roosevelt dryly.

"Well . . . you can see the motive for murdering Philip Garber. If someone believed he had in his possession any very great part of the missing gems, it would afford ample motive for homicide."

"I see no motive in it for Pamela Rush-Hodgeborne to have killed him. Being a principal suspect in the burglary, she could hardly want to take a fortune in stolen jewels into her possession."

"With all due respect," said Sir Rodney, "I am afraid your reasoning follows something other than the laws of pure logic."

"I do have an *instinct* in the matter," said Mrs. Roosevelt. "I readily acknowledge that."

"Ah," said Sir Rodney with a brief nod. "Allow me to pour you another cup of tea."

5

July mornings could be oppressive in Washington—hot, damp, and close. Mrs. Roosevelt remembered with some amusement that the British still paid their diplomats extra money while they were stationed in Washington. It was regarded by London as a hardship station—a subtropical climate. Though she was dressed for it—in a loose, flowing white dress with blue polka dots, and comfortable white low-heeled shoes—still the heat wore on her and depressed her mood.

She was in her office, working on her newspaper column, when the call came from Missy.

"Mrs. Roosevelt, would you mind coming down to the Oval Office? The President would like to see you."

She was busy. The "Pamela problem" was taking too much of her time, and she was behind on the column, her correspondence, and half a dozen other things. But of course a call from the President was a call from the President. She hurried down and out to the West Wing.

Missy was waiting. "Director Hoover is with the President," she cautioned.

Mrs. Roosevelt wrinkled her nose. Then she fixed her smile and walked into the Oval Office.

The President sat behind his cluttered desk, cigarette holder in his teeth. He wore a rumpled tan suit. J. Edgar Hoover, director of the Federal Bureau of Investigation, sat nearby in a white suit, looking dapper and comfortable.

"Edgar has come to offer his assistance with the Pamela Rush-Hodgeborne business," said the President.

Mrs. Roosevelt smiled at the director. "How very kind," she said.

"I hope the Bureau can be of some help to you, Mrs. Roosevelt," aid Hoover smoothly.

"I hope so, too."

"Frank Garber has called on Edgar and asked him to help squelch he rumor that young Garber was somehow involved in a burglary in England," said the President.

"The burglary at Austin House," said Mrs. Roosevelt. "Scotland Yard believes Philip Garber *was* involved."

"Yes," said the director. "And, of course, Scotland Yard believes Miss Rush-Hodgeborne was involved."

Mrs. Roosevelt nodded.

"It would be helpful to establish that neither one of them had anything to do with it," said the director.

"I am afraid that will be more than a little difficult," said Mrs. Roosevelt.

"It might not be," he replied, "if Miss Rush-Hodgeborne will cooperate."

"Of course she will cooperate. What cooperation do you have in mind?"

"I think it could perhaps be arranged," said the director, "for the District court to accept a plea of guilty to some reduced charge—say, manslaughter—on the theory that Miss Rush-Hodgeborne was deeply in love with Philip Garber and killed him when she learned he would not marry her. Temporary insanity, you know. She could be sentenced to a term of a few years, and it could be arranged for her to have a parole after a short time, on condition she leave the country. After all, the United States has no wish to hold the girl in jail."

"All this could be done very silently, I suppose," said Mrs. Roosevelt.

Hoover nodded. "We would hear no more about the Earl of Crittenden's jewels, no more about the possibility that Philip Garber and Pamela Rush-Hodgeborne were themselves the Austin House burglars."

"That is, naturally, what Frank Garber wants," said the President.

"I am a little surprised, even at Congressman Garber, that he should find this solution to the case attractive," said Mrs. Roosevelt.

"Why?" asked the director. "His son is dead. He can't bring him back, but he would like to preserve his good reputation."

"I should *think*," said Mrs. Roosevelt somewhat loftily, "that he would be curious to know who did in fact kill his son."

"He believes Pamela Rush-Hodgeborne killed him," said the director.

"Do *you* believe she did, Mr. Hoover?"

The director smiled condescendingly. "I understand you think she's not guilty, Mrs. Roosevelt."

"I don't just think so. I *know* it," said she.

"Nevertheless, the evidence against her is quite compelling. She might be very well advised to consider pleading to a lesser charge. Poisoning carries the death penalty, you know. The law regards it very seriously."

"As it does what I believe in legal terminology is called 'burglary of an inhabited dwelling house in the night season,'" said Mrs. Roosevelt.

Hoover frowned. "It is not," he said, cautiously choosing his words, "impossible that Scotland Yard is wrong in suspecting either of these two young people. As I understand it, their suspicion is based principally on the idea that some of the jewels from the Crittenden collection have been fenced here in the United States. If the fence—who is in jail in New York now—were to testify that he got those jewels from a London hoodlum fresh off the boat, that would, uh . . ."

"That could be arranged? I mean, the fence might remember that was how he got the jewels?"

The director shrugged. "Perhaps."

"I see."

"Miss Rush-Hodgeborne would not, then, have to go home to face trial on a burglary charge—after serving her term here."

"How very tidy," said Mrs. Roosevelt.

"Well, I thought you might want to tell Miss Rush-Hodgeborne that some such alternative may become available to her."

"I certainly will tell her," said Mrs. Roosevelt. "She should know."

"Then I . . . I have a request of you, Mrs. Roosevelt," said the director.

"I hope I shall be able to accommodate you," said she, smiling.

He nodded. "Thank you. Since, from this point forward, the in quiry will be picked up by the Bureau, with competent agents assigned to look into every element of the case, it would be helpful to us if you would, uh, abstain from your own inquiries. If for no other reason, Mrs. Roosevelt, I should point out to you that your interest in the matter could generate an extraordinary quantity of publicity, which could impede our efforts."

"And distress Frank Garber," she added.

"Well . . ."

She turned to the President. "Do you join in this request?" she asked.

The President shrugged and turned up his palms. "I? All I am is a reluctant witness to this conversation," he said, his cigarette holder wobbling in his teeth as he spoke. "If you and Edgar can work something out, it will be all right with me."

"I will communicate your suggestion to Pamela, Director Hoover," said Mrs. Roosevelt.

When Hoover left, she remained alone with the President.

"How much longer do you mean to tolerate that man?" she asked.

"If I fired him, it would create another fight with the Congress— over not much," said the President. "I have more important battles up there. Suppose getting rid of Hoover cost me votes on the Neutrality Act repeal?"

She shook her head. "Politics," she murmured distastefully.

"Politics, *right!*" He laughed. "And you love 'em, old girl! You like politics better than I do. Don't deny it."

She sighed. "Pamela is innocent, Franklin."

"I don't doubt it."

"I will ask you to take action in her case, if necessary."

"Let's hope it doesn't become necessary. For more reasons than one."

The President reached to the table behind his desk and handed her a newspaper—the New York *Daily News*.

"Look at page four," he said.

She looked at a story that someone had marked with a pen.

> Eleanor Roosevelt is at it again. She seems to have made the defense of her English-born secretary, Pamela Rush-

Hodgeborne, charged in the poison murder of the son of New Jersey Congressman Frank Garber, another of her causes. The First Lady has been seen visiting the girl at the District of Columbia jail. The rumor is that she is playing detective, too, looking for evidence to prove the beauteous Pamela did not spike Philip Garber's Old Fashioned cocktail with potassium cyanide. Never has there been a more irregular Baker Street irregular. Have at it, Mrs. R.! The game is afoot!

The President watched her scan the story. "It argues for circumspection," he said when he saw her look up from the page. "Too much publicity can harm Pamela."

Mrs. Roosevelt nodded as she handed the newspaper back to him. "Franklin," she said, "I am practically certain that Philip Garber was a participant in the Austin House burglary. I am practically certain, too, that Pamela was not, but that he used her, not only to gain access to the earl and to his house, but also to carry away his share of the loot."

"Be careful, Babs," said the President. "What do you gain by proving that? All you do is give the police her motive for murdering Garber."

"Not at all, ma'am," said Captain Kennelly. "I will always have time for *you*. Make yourself comfortable, if you can in this heat. We're slowly learning more about the Garber and Rush-Hodgeborne case."

"Anything good for poor Pamela?" asked Mrs. Roosevelt.

He shook his head. "I'm afraid I can't characterize anything we've learned as good news for her," he said. "I believe you have been told that the diamond I showed you—the one we found in her watch—has been identified as a diamond stolen in the English burglary."

"Yes. I've been told that."

"All of the diamonds fenced in New York are of a size that would have fit inside the channel in the watch," he added ominously. "It seems very likely that Miss Rush-Hodgeborne entered this country carrying a fortune in stolen gems in her lapel watch."

"Is it possible for me to examine the watch?"

He shrugged. "Certainly. Why not?"

Kennelly unlocked the drawer of his steel desk and took out the big white envelope she had seen before. He removed the watch and handed it to her.

"Show me how to open it, please," she said.

The captain took the watch back. "It's quite simple," he said. "The back unscrews. You just put your fingers on it firmly, like this, and turn."

She tried it. The back turned smoothly.

"Opens like any pocket watch, just about," said Captain Kennelly.

"Of course, you wouldn't open it as long as the watch was running properly and did not require repair," said Mrs. Roosevelt.

"You're suggesting she did not open it, that someone else put the jewels in and took them out, and that she didn't know it," said Kennelly. "That someone else of course has to be Philip Garber."

"Why not?" asked Mrs. Roosevelt.

The captain clasped the fingers of his big hands and pressed them to his chin. "Then why did she kill him?" he asked.

"She didn't," said Mrs. Roosevelt simply.

"But he's dead," said the captain.

"Someone else killed him."

"By having her poison him? Really, ma'am, isn't it much more likely that they stole the jewels, that she smuggled them into this country in the watch, and that they quarreled over the money he got when he fenced them—and that for that reason she killed him? That's what a jury is going to believe."

"I fear so," she sighed. "But, Captain, where are the rest of the jewels?"

"Where they hid them, in England. Or in the hands of confederates."

Mrs. Roosevelt closed her eyes momentarily. "A jury *is* going to believe that, isn't it, Captain Kennelly?"

"Yes, ma'am. It doesn't look at all good for the girl. Besides that, I have something else that doesn't look good for her, either."

"Oh? What now?"

"It turns out that Philip Garber was making plans to be married soon—but not to Pamela Rush-Hodgeborne. It seems that we have a new motive. Jealousy."

"Would you give me the facts?"

"Yes, ma'am. Have you ever heard of a place called The New Club? It's an illegal gambling club over in Fairfax County."

"No, I'm quite sure I've never heard of it."

Captain Kennelly allowed himself a smile. "I didn't suppose you had, ma'am. It's located in a fine old country house, surrounded by fields. They serve the finest food and drink, but the chief attraction is the gambling—cards, dice, roulette . . . everything. You have to pay five hundred dollars to join. Philip Garber was a member. In the month before his death, he lost more than a thousand dollars at the gambling tables. His salary at the White House was forty dollars a week."

"Maybe his father gave him the money. But what does this have to do with his planning to marry?"

"His father vehemently denies he gave him that kind of money. Anyway, the New Club is where Philip met the girl he wanted to marry. It's a place where a lot of young people of her class go."

"And what class is that?"

"Her name is Cynthia Dawes. Her family is quite wealthy. Hunt-club people. First family of Virginia and all that. Cynthia is quite beautiful, I might add."

"Captain Kennelly," said Mrs. Roosevelt, "are you aware that Frank Garber is little better than a gangster—in fact may be one? It is difficult to imagine that Philip Garber would have been received in the home of these hunt-club, F.F.V. people, much less be allowed to court their daughter."

"He was not received in their home. Robert Dawes didn't know about Philip Garber." The captain hesitated. "I'm afraid the fact is, ma'am, that young people today live by standards you and I find . . . well, personally, I find them shocking."

"So you think Pamela might have killed Philip out of jealousy over Cynthia Dawes?"

"Mrs. Roosevelt," said the captain grimly, "I think Philip and Pamela stole the earl's diamonds, either alone or with the help of someone in England. I think Pamela smuggled some of the stones into this country in her watch. I think Philip fenced those stones and got a lot of money—which he immediately began to spend on high living, including membership in The New Club, where he met Cynthia Dawes. I think he was cheating Pamela out of her share of the money. I think she knew that, and when she found out besides that he was seeing Cynthia and planning to marry her, she killed him. I'm sorry, ma'am, but that's what I think."

Mrs. Roosevelt sighed unhappily. "I would like to talk with Pamela," she said.

"Well, it's visiting hours now. The visiting room is full of people. I can have her brought here, I guess. Or you can see her inside the jail. Her cell is at the near end of the row. No one else would need to see you visiting her there."

"I would like to see the conditions under which she is imprisoned."

A rattling old oscillating fan blew air in from the window and along the row of cells. It blew none into the cells, though, and Pamela's gray prison dress was damp and wrinkled. Her brow glistened with sweat. She stood and reached through the heavy, close-set bars to touch Mrs. Roosevelt's hand; then she sank down wearily on the bunk that hung from two chains on one wall of the cell.

"Oh, child," said Mrs. Roosevelt, shaking her head. "How *awful* for you!"

" 'Tis awful, isn't it?" said Pamela.

"I shall see to it that some things are sent you. I shall have a basket delivered here this afternoon. Some fruit. Some books. And—"

"Some soap, please," said Pamela.

A woman in a cell down the line rattled her cell door and howled. She demanded that whoever was out there come back and let her out.

Pamela glanced in the direction of the howling prisoner. "She says she's not who they think she is. And maybe she isn't."

"Pamela," said Mrs. Roosevelt. "The police think you and Philip stole the earl's jewels, that you smuggled some of them into this country in your watch, that you and he quarreled over the money he obtained for them, and that you killed him."

"Have you begun to think so, too, Mrs. Roosevelt?" asked Pamela despondently.

"No. Not at all. But I want you to know there is a possibility they will offer you the option of pleading guilty to a lesser charge, like manslaughter, so there won't have to be a trial and the suspicion that

Philip was a thief won't be aired. You would wind up spending a few years in prison, after which you would be deported."

"I am not guilty, Mrs. Roosevelt," said Pamela firmly.

Mrs. Roosevelt nodded. "I know you are not. You must realize, though, that you risk a life sentence, or the death penalty, if you insist on going to trial."

"If I go meekly to prison for a crime I did not commit," said Pamela, "then the person who did kill Philip will go free. Who is offering me this 'opportunity'?"

"His father is behind it."

"Then maybe *he* had someone put poison in my bottle of bitters."

"The thought has occurred to me."

"What would *you* do, Mrs. Roosevelt? Would you plead guilty to a lesser charge?"

Mrs. Roosevelt stiffened, raised her chin. "I would not, Pamela," she said. "I would not, but I cannot insist that you do not." She paused. "In any event, the option has not been offered. If and when it is, we will get you a lawyer. Now I have some questions."

"Can't they bring you a chair?" asked Pamela.

"I told them not to."

She stood just outside Pamela's cell, resting her right hand on the crossbar of the door. In the hurry of the day a wisp of her hair had got loose and hung over her left ear. She pulled a handkerchief from her sleeve and wiped her brow.

"I want you to think, Pamela," she said. "You told me Philip brought a bottle of cognac to your room the night of the burglary. Was that bottle still in your room when you woke in the morning?"

Pamela frowned. "I don't remember," she said. "It was a confused, difficult time, you know."

"Scotland Yard says it did not find any bottle of cognac in your room that morning."

"Really? I wonder . . . ?"

Mrs. Roosevelt watched the girl ponder, giving her time to think through the implication. "Do you see, Pamela?" she said then. "Do you see what it suggests?"

Pamela nodded. "That Philip got up in the middle of the night and went downstairs. He returned the brandy and . . ."

"Yes."

"*I suspected it!* I've suspected it all along. I couldn't bring myself to think . . . Oh, and when he dropped his chips on my feet in Hyde Park, it was an artifice, then! He wanted to meet me and use me to gain entry to the earl's house and the earl's presence! Oh! And he took my watch downstairs with him that night, and he hid diamonds in it! And . . . Oh, Mrs. Roosevelt! Almost all that the police suspect is true!" Pamela rose and stood at the bars. Her face had turned red.

"Pamela," said Mrs. Roosevelt quietly. "Is there anything more about Philip that you want to tell me now?"

Pamela frowned deeply. "How did he get the safe open?" she asked.

"Easily enough," said Mrs. Roosevelt. "A safe like that one is not hard to open. But what did he do with the rest of the stolen jewels? The ones that came over in your lapel watch amounted to no more than a fraction of what was taken."

"I've no idea."

"He had accomplices," said Mrs. Roosevelt. "One pictures them sitting down in the earl's library and dividing the loot."

"Then who killed him?" asked Pamela. "And why?"

Mrs. Roosevelt shook her head. "I don't know. Indeed, I'm afraid I don't even have any very sound idea."

"Nor have I," said Pamela, sinking down again on her chain-hung bunk.

"Tell me, Pamela—have you ever heard of a girl named Cynthia Dawes?"

Pamela shook her head.

"Have you heard of a place called The New Club?"

Again Pamela shook her head.

"Was Philip a big spender?"

"No, not at all. His salary in the usher's office was only . . . But he must have realized thousands on the sale of the diamonds he took from my watch!"

"Yes. Indeed he did. Your case is becoming more complicated, Pamela. I am going to seek help. I am sorry you have to stay in here, but I shall send a basket. I must go to New York for the weekend, but I'll return on Monday and will see you again. Don't despair, my dear. All is not lost."

6

In most American cities, Mrs. Roosevelt reflected as she looked out the window of her White House office, a hard rain would cool the air and the earth and bring relief from the summer heat. Not in Washington. The very rain seemed as if it had been heated to bath temperature before it fell. The streets steamed after the rain, and the sun beat down through the haze, and the city remained oppressively hot and humid.

There were pickets outside the fence this morning. If they imagined the President took notice—or, in fact, that he could read their signs or understand a word of their shrill shouts—they were mistaken. He had made a rough count of one crowd of pickets and called them "a minority of twenty." Of these there were not twenty.

She worked on her column—"My Day"—discussing the meeting she had had recently with a dozen former CCC boys who had come to Hyde Park to plant a pine tree on the estate as an expression of their gratitude to the President for the Civilian Conservation Corps. They had told her what it meant to them to have had the opportunity to work in the CCC—to eat "three squares every day," as they put it, but more importantly to regain their self-esteem, doing something they saw as useful, productive. She dictated her reflections on the meeting to Miss Weems, who was doing double work now, since Pamela was in jail.

The telephone rang, and Miss Weems answered. "Sir Rodney Harcourt," she said after a moment, and Mrs. Roosevelt took the call.

"Ah, Mrs. Rose-vult," said Sir Rodney in a hearty voice. "I've good news for you in the Rush-Hodgeborne matter. A man has just arrived on the trans-Atlantic clipper—by way of Lisbon, y' know. Sir Alan

Burton. A chief inspector from Scotland Yard. Very eminent investigator. Very eminent."

"Should I have heard the name before?" asked Mrs. Roosevelt.

"Not likely," said Sir Rodney. "*I've* heard of him, but no one else here at the embassy ever had. He's a specialist in confidential investigations, sensitive matters, matters with a potential of embarrassing His Majesty's Government. To be altogether frank with you, I'm amazed that they sent him."

"It's very good of your government."

"Yes. . . . Well, uh, Mrs. Rose-vult, uh, please allow me to emphasize the importance of maintaining his incognito. Officially, he's in Stockholm, looking into the matter of the disappearance of certain embassy funds. Only a few people in London know he's actually in Washington."

"I will keep your government's secret, Sir Rodney."

"Very good. Sir Alan would like an early appointment with you—today if possible."

"I can see him at two," said Mrs. Roosevelt.

Sir Alan Burton was punctual. At two precisely he arrived at the White House and was shown to Mrs. Roosevelt's office. He was a sandy-haired, freckled, stout man, about forty years old, as she judged. He was sweating visibly in his rumpled tweeds.

"Although I am certainly glad to see you," she said to him as soon as he was seated, "I must confess my surprise. I had hardly expected your government to send a man like you."

"The Earl of Crittenden is not without influence," said Sir Alan Burton gravely. "Nor is the fact of *your* interest. His Majesty's Government are—quite unofficially, of course—deeply concerned."

"I am pleased to hear it," said Mrs. Roosevelt. "I hoped your government would recognize an obligation to help Miss Rush-Hodgeborne, and yet I was afraid it wouldn't."

"The matter *is* quite delicate," said Sir Alan. "Since we cannot be sure how your government or your newspapers would receive the idea of Scotland Yard meddling in an American investigation, I am in the States quite unofficially and under strict orders to maintain an incognito. The Foreign Secretary would have preferred that no one come at all."

"And just what do you hope to accomplish?" asked Mrs. Roosevelt.

"The Government regard the Rush-Hodgeborne matter as potentially disastrous to Anglo-American relations," said Sir Alan. "The father of Philip Garber is, after all, a member not just of your Congress but, as we understand, a leading member of an important Congressional committee. If Philip Garber took part in the Austin House burglary, we want to prove it by ironclad evidence—we want either that or to clear his name and drop the matter."

Mrs. Roosevelt clasped her hands together and regarded the inspector with marked skepticism. "What outcome of the case would please you most?" she asked.

Sir Alan coughed and frowned. "To learn that neither young Mr. Garber nor Miss Rush-Hodgeborne had anything to do with the burglary and that Miss Rush-Hodgeborne did not kill Philip Garber."

"I am afraid you are asking for too much," said Mrs. Roosevelt. "I believe you will have to settle for half of it."

"That Philip Garber was one of the Austin House burglars but that Miss Rush-Hodgeborne did not kill him?"

Mrs. Roosevelt nodded.

"Then who did, Mrs. Roosevelt?" asked Sir Alan.

"I am hoping you will help me find out," she said, with a smile.

"Yes, of course," said Sir Alan. "In fact, you asked for some information from Scotland Yard files. I have it."

"Very good."

"You understand, of course, that I was not involved in the investigation-in-chief. I was engaged in quite another investigation at the time. What I tell you is what I've learned from my reading of the file."

"I understand."

"The Yard inspectors who were assigned to the case were at great pains to learn all they could about young Mr. Garber's activities in England during his residence there. Please understand, too, that if, uh—if the facts I am about to disclose do not become essential to our investigation here, it would be better if they remained confidential."

Mrs. Roosevelt nodded.

"Well, then. Young Mr. Garber was sent to England by his father, to study at Oxford," said Sir Alan, rubbing his hands together lightly, carefully drawing his statement from his memory. "He discontinued those studies not long after he arrived. He was more interested, it seems, in gaming, drinking, and the company of young women of questionable character. In fact, he seems to have associated himself with a variety of persons of the lower sort—I mean persons with no visible, and probably no legitimate, means of earning a living. He spent a good deal. We are not quite sure where his funds came from. He deposited a monthly check from his father in a London bank, and supposedly he lived on that, since he had no other source of income that we know of; but clearly he spent more than his father sent him. Much more."

"He became a thief," said Mrs. Roosevelt simply.

"We have no firm evidence of it," said Sir Alan. "But to continue— in the autumn of last year he ceased to deposit funds from his father in his London bank, and shortly he closed the account by drawing the last money from it. That was still a short time before he took employment with the Earl of Crittenden. The earl paid him ten pounds a week in London, five pounds a week after he took room and board at Austin House. He still came up to London on weekends and frequented his old haunts, spending far more than his five pounds could possibly have supported."

"If he was not stealing the money, then where was he getting it?"

Sir Alan smiled thinly. "I am hoping you can help us find out, Mrs. Roosevelt."

Late that afternoon, she again visited Pamela at the jail. The young woman was despondent. She said she had been questioned for two hours by agents of the Federal Bureau of Investigation, who plainly believed she was guilty, not just of murder, but also of the Austin House burglary. Her spirits were lifted somewhat by the news that a chief inspector from Scotland Yard had come to Washington. She could not, she said apologetically, help but have more confidence in the men from the Yard than she did in American detectives.

The next day, Tuesday, at about noon, Sir Alan—absent his tweeds and nattily dressed in a cream-white linen suit—accompanied Mrs. Roosevelt on a drive over into Fairfax County. She refused to allow Secret Service agents to accompany her or anyone to drive her. She herself drove a 1936 Plymouth that belonged to Harry Hopkins, and her initial difficulty with the clutch made the chief inspector nervous during all the rest of the drive. From Captain Kennelly she had obtained directions to The New Club, and after missing turns three times, she and Sir Alan finally reached the big white frame farmhouse at about one-thirty.

Even in midafternoon there were a dozen cars parked around the house, including several Cadillacs and Packards. Getting out of the car, she slapped some of the wrinkles out of her pink dress, adjusted her white straw hat, and led the bemused Sir Alan Burton toward the stone steps to the broad front porch. She found the door locked, but there was a knocker, and she rapped authoritatively.

The door was opened a crack, to the limit allowed by a chain. "Are you a member, madame?" asked a cold voice.

"Are you the owner or manager?" she asked.

"Madame, are you a member of the club?" the voice asked impatiently.

"I am Mrs. Eleanor Roosevelt, and I wish to speak with the owner or manager," she said.

An eye appeared in the crack. It peered at her for a moment. "Please wait," said the voice.

A minute later, a large man with slick, brilliantined black hair and a black pencil mustache, dressed in a crisp white suit, white shirt, and black bow tie, opened the door wide and smiled expansively. "Mrs. Roosevelt, it is you indeed!" he said in a happy voice. "What an honor! Please come in. Come in!"

In the minute he had been given, the man obviously had ordered all the doors off the entrance hall tightly closed, and he led Mrs. Roosevelt and Sir Alan Burton down a long carpeted hall toward the rear of the house. He opened a door and preceded them into a small but comfortable office, furnished with a mahogany desk and leather chairs; he invited them to be seated and asked them what they would like to drink.

"A cold lemonade would be very pleasant," said Mrs. Roosevelt.

"Of course. And for you, sir?"

"Whisky," said Sir Alan.

A black servant, who had appeared in the doorway, had overheard their orders and departed quietly.

"Let me introduce myself," said the man before he sat down behind his desk. "I am Peter McIntosh. I own The New Club. I am honored to welcome you."

"This is Sir Alan Burton, from the British Embassy," said Mrs. Roosevelt.

"How do you do?" said McIntosh. "I am, as I say, honored to welcome you both—but, I must confess, I am also mystified. To what do I owe the pleasure?"

"We have come to inquire about Philip Garber," said Mrs. Roosevelt.

McIntosh nodded, and his face darkened. "Oh, yes. The police have asked about him, too."

"What I should like to know," said Mrs. Roosevelt bluntly, yet with an innocent smile, "is how much money he spent here."

"I'm afraid I can't say," said McIntosh smoothly. "He spent cash. I don't know how much."

"You must have some idea," she persisted.

McIntosh shrugged. "It would be a matter of a thousand dollars or more. As much as two thousand, maybe."

"In cash," said Sir Alan thoughtfully. "You accepted no checks, extended no credit?"

"I am sure you understand that my operation here is illegal, Sir Alan," said McIntosh with disarming candor. "I don't take checks. I extend credit only to a few preferred clients."

"Oh, Mr. McIntosh," said Mrs. Roosevelt, with a broad smile, "I have friends who have paid their obligations to you with checks."

She had ventured a complete lie, on an impulse, and now she hoped he would not ask her who those friends were.

McIntosh smiled. Probably he understood. "I took no checks from Garber, just the same," he said. "I suppose the police will look at his bank records. They'll find no checks he wrote here."

"Why not?" asked Sir Alan.

McIntosh turned up the palms of his hands. "I didn't trust him," he said, without allowing the slightest diminution of his smile.

"Good," said Mrs. Roosevelt. "You were well advised. Now tell me about Cynthia Dawes."

McIntosh's forehead wrinkled, but he still smiled. "You ask difficult questions, Mrs. Roosevelt. I try to make it a point to preserve my clients' confidences. What do you want me to tell you about Miss Dawes?"

"Is she a member?"

"Her father is a member."

"Does she come here alone?"

"No, with friends."

"With her father?"

"No."

"Do you extend credit to her?"

"Yes."

Mrs. Roosevelt returned his smile. The door opened then, and the servant brought in their drinks. She sipped her tart, cold lemonade before she returned to her questions.

"Did Philip Garber and Cynthia Dawes meet here?"

McIntosh sighed. "Both of them enjoyed gambling. Both of them liked to drink—"

"What did Philip drink, Mr. McIntosh?" she interrupted to ask.

"Old Fashioneds. Nothing but Old Fashioneds."

"That was observed?" she asked.

"I suppose so. He made a point of it."

"Very well. Then tell me, Mr. McIntosh, what was the nature of the relationship between Philip Garber and Cynthia Dawes?"

"I—I am going to refuse to answer, Mrs. Roosevelt. I am terribly sorry. I don't mean to be rude. But it is a matter I cannot discuss."

"Can you tell me where I will find Cynthia's father?"

"Certainly. He's a lawyer in Falls Church."

Three-quarters of an hour later they sat across the desk from Robert Dawes, a big, pipe-smoking, fifty-year-old man with a solid, square, florid face.

"It is very difficult," he said, speaking in the precise, decelerated tones of an aristocratic Southern accent, "t' refuse to see the First Lady. But I will tell you, Mrs. Roosevelt, I would not see you if you were not the First Lady. I have no desire ever again t' hear the name Philip Garber. I am glad he is dead. If I have any regret, it is that I did not kill him myself."

"Oh!" said Mrs. Roosevelt, shocked. "There must be something dreadful behind a statement like that."

Dawes set his jaw. "He came down here," he growled, "from N' Jersey—certainly one of the sinkholes of the world. I understand his father is a ward heeler, nothin' better than a gangster. That boy brought his own kind of standards with him—and he applied 'em here."

"Did he . . . do something wrong to your daughter?" asked Sir Alan.

"My daughter, sir, has her own fortune—inherited from her grandmother. He wished t' get his hands on it, I have no doubt. He could have lived in th' *economic* circumstances of a gentleman thereafter— though nothin' would ever have made him one."

"Then he . . . ?" asked Mrs. Roosevelt, unwilling to finish the question but knowing Dawes would understand what she was asking.

"He dishonored her," said Dawes grimly. "I wouldn't tell you, but it's known. McIntosh allowed 'em to use a room upstairs at his place."

"I am very sorry, Mr. Dawes," said Mrs. Roosevelt. "We know Philip Garber was a despicable person."

" 'Despicable' is not a strong enough word, Mrs. Roosevelt," said Dawes. "Not only did he dishonor my little girl, he humiliated her."

"Oh, dear."

"He attempted to set up a place of *assignation* for 'em in Washin'ton. In the apartment of that other poor young woman he dishonored."

"Do you mean *Pamela*, Mr. Dawes?"

"Yes, ma'am. The poor girl that's in jail for killin' him."

"He wanted your daughter to come to Pamela's apartment?"

Dawes nodded emphatically. "He gave her a key and told her she could meet him there and spend the night with him."

"But Pamela . . . She would have been there."

"No, ma'am. Th' other young woman would have been in N' York, with you—on some kind of trip she took with you. That's what he wanted my daughter to do: to come spend the night in another girl's apartment, for his—his sordid purposes."

"Cynthia refused, I suppose?"

"Cynthia was . . . was *shattered*. She hadn't known he had an illicit relationship with *another*."

"Oh, dear," said Mrs. Roosevelt again. She looked into the frowning face of Sir Alan Burton. *"Oh, dear!"*

7

The President shook his martinis with his accustomed vigor and talked with Missy and Harry Hopkins.

"I am sorry," Missy said to him, "that we couldn't have found some way to spare you from Frank Garber this afternoon. He would not be put off. He insisted he had to see you."

"Well, he is not the grieving father," said the President. "I offered him my condolences on the death of his son, and he just shrugged that off and launched into his complaint."

"Which is?" asked Hopkins, drawing deeply on his cigarette.

"Which of course is," said the President, "that Babs is conducting her own personal crusade to win acquittal for Pamela Rush-Hodge-borne."

"Does he believe the girl is guilty?" Missy asked.

"Absolutely. He says his son had been trying to rid himself of the girl for months but that she clung to him and wouldn't let him end an affair he was tired of. That's a bald-faced lie, of course. If the boy wanted to rid himself of Pamela, why did he use his father's political influence to get himself a job here in the White House, where she worked and would be close to him every day?"

"Why would Frank lie?" asked Hopkins.

"I'd like to know. I really would," said the President. "The least sinister motive I can think of is that he simply wants to close the matter as expeditiously as possible, to prevent disclosure of the fact that his son was suspected of burglary in England."

"He's recruited Edgar Hoover to do that for him," said Missy.

"He came close to threatening me," said the President. "He said Babs was going to win herself some bad and costly publicity if she persevered in interfering in a police and F.B.I. investigation. It will be deeply resented in New Jersey, he said, 'when the New York papers tell the extent of her meddling.' " The President grinned. "He assumes I'm going to run for a third term next year. He assumes I'm worried about support from his organization."

Missy had the glasses ready, and the President poured a martini for himself and one for Hopkins. She poured her Scotch, and the three of them lifted their glasses in mutual salute.

"Did the British ambassador say anything about the Rush-Hodgeborne matter?" Hopkins asked.

The President laughed. "Lord Lothian spoke of nothing else. That's why he came to see me—to express his government's deep concern about the murder of Philip Garber. With Europe on the brink of war, the British ambassador called on the President of the United States to convey his Prime Minister's regrets that a British subject apparently has murdered the son of what he called 'a leading member of the United States Congress.' "

Hopkins frowned and shook his head.

"Actually, of course," the President went on, "what really worries them is Babs. They are not quite sure what it signifies that the wife of the President has involved herself so personally in the investigation of a crime. They tend to assume she is acting for me—the old story of Babs being my eyes and ears."

"She would be well advised to back off the matter," said Hopkins.

"Yes. So why don't you tell her so, Harry?"

Hopkins smiled wryly. "I'll leave that to you," he said.

The President sipped from his cold, pungent martini. "It seems that Horace Wilson has looked into the case and advised Neville Chamberlain on it. As a consequence, the British government has a 'policy' on the matter, at least unofficially."

"Which is?" asked Missy.

"His Majesty's Government," said the President with mock gravity, "deeply regret that one of His Majesty's subjects, placed in the employ of the First Lady on the recommendation of one of His Majesty's most prominent subjects, should have murdered the son of a leading member of the United States Congress. And so forth and so on. Their interest is the same as Frank Garber's—to settle the matter quickly and quietly."

"That's why they've sent the man from Scotland Yard, I suppose," said Missy.

"Lord Lothian didn't say it in so many words," the President continued, "but I think he meant me to understand that his government wishes Babs were not so interested in the case. The Scotland Yard man, I think, is not here to help Babs find out who killed Philip Garber: He's here to convince her Pamela did it. He's going to look at whatever evidence she digs up, maybe on the pretense of helping her, and then show her how little it weighs in comparison to the evidence against Pamela. That's my judgment, anyway. He's here to discourage Babs."

Harry Hopkins laughed. "Obviously they don't know Mrs. Roosevelt."

The President laughed, too—a hearty, healthy laugh. "They'll learn," he said.

In Fairfax County, Mrs. Roosevelt and Sir Alan Burton had returned to The New Club, and at this moment they stood staring into a closet in the office of the proprietor, Robert McIntosh. McIntosh, in the closet, held a curtain apart, and they peered through a two-way mirror into the smoke-blue gaming room on the other side.

"The brunette in red is Cynthia Dawes," said McIntosh in a hushed voice. "Playing blackjack."

In a form-fitting red silk dress, the young woman slouched at the table, and the fluid look in her eyes suggested she had perhaps already had too much to drink, although it was only the beginning of the evening. She held a cigarette between her lips as she lifted the corner of her face-down card and reassured herself, apparently, that it was indeed the card she thought it was. She was young, but her face was hard; her posture and air—so far as they could be judged through the glass—were burdened and cynical. She gestured to the dealer, and he slapped down a second face-up card in front of her. She said something that could not be heard through the mirror and picked up her glass and took a drink of what appeared to be whiskey, perhaps with soda, as she waited for the game to go around. Lifting her chin and blowing cigarette smoke toward the lamp over the table, she tipped her head and watched impatiently as the dealer dealt cards to the two other players. She watched them lose. Finally the dealer dealt to himself. He turned over his cards and dealt one. Eighteen. Cynthia Dawes turned over her cards. Nineteen. With a sneer she pulled her chips across the table.

"Daddy's little girl," said McIntosh sarcastically. He let the curtain fall together and cover the mirror as he stepped out of the closet and closed the door. "So," he said. "That's Cynthia Dawes. Are you satisfied?"

"I should like to ask a number of additional questions," said Mrs. Roosevelt.

"Well, I don't know. You put me in an extremely awkward position," complained McIntosh.

"Not nearly so awkward, my dear fellow," said Sir Alan Burton, "as the one in which we shall place you if you do not extend your complete cooperation."

McIntosh breathed deeply and ran his finger along his thin black mustache. "I guess there is something to that," he conceded.

They had telephoned him after they left the law office of Robert Dawes. He had agreed to receive them at a rear door of the club, so they could enter without being seen—which, they discovered when they arrived, was not an unusual way to enter The New Club. The evening was beginning, and McIntosh was wearing a double-breasted white dinner jacket.

"Mr. Dawes is most unhappy with you, Mr. McIntosh," said Mrs. Roosevelt. "He blames you in part for what happened between his daughter and Philip Garber."

"Yes, he hasn't been back in the club since he found out about Cynthia and Philip," said McIntosh.

"But *she* still comes?"

"All the time," said McIntosh. "She has her own money, and she is, after all, of age. But Cynthia's not the blushing flower her father seems to think she is."

"You rented her a room in which she and Philip, uh, pursued their amours," said Sir Alan.

McIntosh nodded at the rotund, florid, sandy-haired Englishman. "That's what I didn't want to talk about this afternoon," he said. "Since her father seems to have told you, though, I see no reason why I should try to keep the secret. I do have three rooms upstairs, which people take when they want to meet privately. They can have food and drink brought up. They can spend the evening or the night. Cynthia Dawes and Philip Garber spent evenings in one of those rooms."

"When did this sort of thing begin, and how often did it happen?" asked Mrs. Roosevelt.

McIntosh shrugged. "Ahh, I guess they first rented a room about the first of May," he said. "They did it once or twice a week."

"Until . . . ?"

"Until about a week before Garber was killed," said McIntosh.

"Is tonight the first time she has been in the club since Garber died?" asked Sir Alan.

"Not at all," said McIntosh. "She was here the night the stories that he had been murdered were in the newspapers. She comes not every night but every other night, I suppose, at least for a drink and a few games of blackjack. She meets her friends here."

"She came more often, then, than Philip Garber?"

"Oh, sure. He never came more often than twice a week."

"Has Cynthia ever spent an evening or a night in a room with any other man?" asked Sir Alan.

"No. I got the impression she fell pretty hard for Garber. I think he worked on that. I think he wanted her money."

"Her father," said Mrs. Roosevelt, "says she was 'shattered' when she learned Philip had a similar relationship with Pamela Rush-Hodgeborne. Did you see any evidence of that?"

McIntosh laughed. " 'Shattered,' " he said. "She nearly shattered him! She threw a champagne bottle at him."

"Indeed? When did this happen? Tell us about it."

"I might as well," said McIntosh, with a careless shrug. "It was an ugly scene, but it's no secret. Others saw it, and you can find out about it if you ask around. So . . . The last time Garber was here— like I said, about a week before he was killed—he and Cynthia had a roaring brawl. It started upstairs. You could hear her screaming at him. Everyone here heard it. There was some banging and thumping. She was throwing things at him. He came running down the stairs, and she came to the top—not entirely dressed, just wearing a black slip—and threw a half-full bottle of champagne at him. It hit him on the shoulder, and champagne flew all over him and all over the wall and carpeting. He never lost a step. He ran right out the front door, got in his car, and drove off, and I never saw him again. It was an ugly scene. I don't like to have things like that happen in the club."

"What was she saying when she was screaming at him?" asked Mrs. Roosevelt.

"Only calling him every name she could lay her tongue to," said McIntosh.

"Did you tell the police about this?" asked Mrs. Roosevelt.

"No. They didn't ask, and I didn't tell them."

"They asked if Philip Garber had owed you money, though, didn't they?"

"Philip Garber did *not* owe me money, Mrs. Roosevelt," said McIntosh quickly, emphatically. "I did not give him credit, just like I told you this afternoon. I didn't trust him. I don't have a marker of Philip Garber's. Not one. Not for a dime."

"I can understand your insistence on that point," said Sir Alan. "After all, we do know something of the tactics employed by gaming clubs to collect their debts."

McIntosh scowled at the Englishman. "I didn't muscle the boy," he said. "I didn't have to. He didn't owe me."

"It seems odd," said Sir Alan, "that you refused credit to a young man, the son of a congressman, who spent as much money with you as Philip Garber did."

"Well, that's the way it was," McIntosh insisted.

"When he first appeared at your door and applied for membership in your gaming club," said Sir Alan, "you made inquiries, I imagine. You made a few telephone calls, did you not? That's what a London club would do. I mean, you would not have let him in at all unless you knew something about him. By your inquiries you learned that Philip Garber had left—what do you call them?—markers at other clubs. And you learned he hadn't paid them. Am I not right?"

"You're *guessing!*" exclaimed McIntosh with a grin.

"Quite," said Sir Alan. "But accurately, it would seem. I think we can relieve you of your anxieties, Mr. McIntosh, if you will just be so good as to give us the names of the other gaming clubs where your inquiries produced the information that young Mr. Garber owed money and hadn't paid."

"You *did* give that information to Congressman Garber, didn't you?" asked Mrs. Roosevelt innocently.

"Yes," said McIntosh sullenly.

"So he *has* been here, then," she said with a smile, pleased that her shot in the dark had hit a target.

McIntosh glared angrily at her. Then he shook his head and conceded her a smile. "You know, if you weren't Mrs. Roosevelt, I'd have you thrown out of here."

"Being First Lady brings a few advantages here and there," she remarked blandly.

"I'm trying to run a quiet place here," said McIntosh. "Strictly honest. I don't cheat at my tables, I don't water the liquor, and I don't let hookers work here. I don't give much credit, like I said, because I don't want collection problems. I can be closed up and run out of the county if I make any trouble. I don't need newspaper stories, either. I'm telling you more than I should because I count on you to be—how do you say?—circumspect."

"Granted, Mr. McIntosh. But to whom did Philip Garber owe money?"

A buzzer sounded on the desk, and McIntosh picked up his telephone. "Ask them to wait a few minutes," he said into the telephone. He turned back toward Mrs. Roosevelt and Sir Alan. "Someone is waiting to see me. I can't keep him waiting long."

"To whom did Philip owe money?" Mrs. Roosevelt persisted.

McIntosh sighed. "Have you ever heard of a club in Maryland called the Kit Kat?"

She shook her head. "No."

"No. Not the kind of place you would know about. It's run by a guy named Gully Balzac. Anything goes with Gully. He's a loan shark. He's a pimp. Philip Garber died owing Gully Balzac thousands of dollars."

"Do you think this Balzac person might have killed Philip Garber, Mr. McIntosh?" asked Mrs. Roosevelt.

McIntosh shook his head. "Gully doesn't say prayers, Mrs. Roosevelt," he said. "But if he did, he'd be thanking God right now that Philip Garber died of poison in a little English girl's apartment. Otherwise, he'd be suspect number one. And number two," he

dded, jerking his thumb toward the closet, "would be the girl sitting
1 there playing blackjack."

"Is that what you told Congressman Garber?" asked Mrs. Rooseelt.

"Not in those words," said McIntosh. He was growing visibly more
npatient, more nervous. "I told you, there's some guys here to see
1e that I can't keep waiting much longer."

Mrs. Roosevelt stood, opened the closet door, pulled back the little
urtain, and peered once more into the smoke-filled gaming room.
Cynthia Garber was still at her table, at the moment shaking a Camel
ut of a crumpled package and—from her look—muttering angrily
ver her cards.

"Why did Frank Garber come here, Mr. McIntosh?" Mrs. Rooseelt asked. "Tell us that, and we can go."

"He wanted to know if his son had owed anything here," said
1cIntosh. "He wanted to settle."

Mrs. Roosevelt squinted, focusing her eyes on a gambler at a table
n the far side of the room. "You *do* have a prominent clientele, Mr.
1cIntosh," she said. "Does Vice President Garner come here often?"
he turned and smiled at McIntosh. "You can't expect us to believe
rank Garber came to volunteer to settle his son's debt to you—
vhich you have said was nonexistent anyway."

"That's why he came, Mrs. Roosevelt," McIntosh declared firmly.

She looked over her shoulder at the white-haired old man with the
ushy eyebrows, gnawing on a cigar and studying his cards. "How
1uch money does the Vice President spend at your tables, Mr. McIn-
osh?"

"What do you want of me?"

She smiled. "Only to know why Frank Garber came here after his
on's death," she said simply.

McIntosh stood. "I think you can guess why. You're good at guess-
ng."

Mrs. Roosevelt's smile broadened. "All right," she said. "I'll play
our game. Congressman Garber did not come here to see you. He
ame to see Cynthia. You arranged a meeting for them."

McIntosh drew a deep breath. "If you already know everything,
vhy do you ask?"

"Why did he want to meet Cynthia Dawes? What did they tal[l] about?"

"Now, *that* I don't know," asserted McIntosh. "And that's for sure They met upstairs, in the room where she used to spend her tim[e] with Philip. I don't have the faintest idea what they talked about, an[d] that's the truth."

"I guess I can believe that," said Mrs. Roosevelt.

"Listen," said McIntosh. "You've gotta go. I told you, guys are here to see me. From the F.B.I. You don't want them to see you here. [I] don't want them to see you here. I can get you out the back door maybe. Just maybe."

"Very well," said Mrs. Roosevelt, casting a last glance into the gaming room, where a new party of guests had just arrived. "I don'[t] particularly want—"

She was interrupted by a loud crash. The door to the office splin tered and swung in, and a young man in a beige suit, wearing a ta[n] straw hat, stumbled into the room, half stunned. He was followed b[y] a bizarre figure nattily dressed in a white suit, with a white straw ha[t] and white-and-black shoes, casually displaying a Thompson sub machine gun cradled in his arms.

"Hands up!" he barked at McIntosh and Sir Alan Burton. He di[d] not see Mrs. Roosevelt in the closet. "I'm Tolson of the F.B.I."

J. Edgar Hoover strolled into the room, dressed similarly in a white suit, white straw hat, white-and-black shoes. "Who are you?" he demanded gruffly of Sir Alan Burton.

"Mr. Hoover," said the First Lady, stepping out of the closet. "Le[t] me introduce Chief Inspector Sir Alan Burton, of Scotland Yard."

Hoover stood with dropped jaw, eyes wide. "Mrs. *Roosevelt!*" he gasped.

"I should be curious," she said, "to know what—other than your obsession with melodrama—justifies your breaking down Mr. McIntosh's door. We should have been finished here in another min ute, and Mr. McIntosh would have seen you then. Really, Mr. Hoo ver, your conduct is inexcusable."

"This is an official investigation," said Tolson. "The director—"

She cut him off with an impatient flutter of her hand. *"Please,* Mr.

Hoover," she said. "Please wait outside until Sir Alan and I have finished our talk with Mr. McIntosh." She cast a hostile glance at Tolson. "And make your disgusting friend put away that big ugly gun."

8

"May I assume, Captain Kennelly, that you have kept a record of every entry of this flat since the arrival of the first police officer on the night of the crime?"

The chief of detectives nodded at Sir Alan Burton. "Yes, Sir Burton," he said.

"You can tell me the name of everyone who has been here, when he was here, and so forth?"

"Right. I've got a notebook with all that in it. The place has been under police seal since that night."

Sir Alan nodded, frowned, and continued to look around the tiny apartment.

Mrs. Roosevelt was even more intensely interested, but she walked in and out of the little bedroom and the little kitchen, and looked into the bathroom, with a sense of intrusion. Pamela Rush-Hodgeborne had lived modestly here. Her clothes still hung in the closet, and Mrs. Roosevelt was surprised to see how few dresses she had.

"The girl smokes?" asked Sir Alan, pointing at an olive-green package of Lucky Strike cigarettes that lay on the small table before the couch.

"Philip Garber smoked Luckies," said Captain Kennelly. "We checked that."

"Two toothbrushes," observed Sir Alan, looking into the bathroom.

"Not only that," said Captain Kennelly. "Two kinds of toothpaste. Ipana and Pepsodent. When Garber stayed here, he wanted things his way."

One of Pamela's few luxuries, Mrs. Roosevelt observed, was a portable electric Victrola and a small collection of records. Looking through the modest stack of discs—"The Music Goes 'Round and 'Round" by Tommy Dorsey and His Clambake Seven, "Three Little Fishies" by Kay Kyser, "Ciribiribin" by Harry James, "A Tisket A Tasket" by Chuck Webb, and so on—she wondered if they reflected Pamela's taste or Philip's.

They looked in the kitchen closet where Pamela had kept whiskey and the fatal bottle of bitters. That was gone, taken by the police. All they saw there now was a bag of Eight O'Clock coffee and a few cans of vegetables.

The apartment was at the rear of the building. The living-room window looked out on an alley.

"You've of course checked the windows and doors for signs of forced entry," said Sir Alan.

"Sure, Sir Burton," said Captain Kennelly. "Normal procedure. These old windows may have been forced in the past, but they've got no fresh marks on 'em."

Sir Alan opened the door into the hall. "Not much of a lock," he said. "We could come in easily enough, couldn't we? Have you had the lock apart, Captain?"

"No. No, we haven't. What do you think we might find inside the lock?"

"Well, let's see, if you don't mind," said Sir Alan, taking out a heavy pocketknife and unfolding a blunt-tipped blade.

As the Washington detective and Mrs. Roosevelt watched, the Scotland Yard detective unscrewed the fastenings of the lock and removed it from the door. Then, on the kitchen table, he disassembled the lock and peered intently at the inner workings.

"Do you see what I do?" he asked Kennelly.

"Scratches," said Captain Kennelly.

"Not made by the key," said Sir Alan. "Made by a pick. Someone has picked this lock. Recently, too. In time, the metal exposed by the scratching would corrode and take the same color as the rest of this brass. These scratches are bright. Someone has broken into this flat within the past few weeks."

Captain Kennelly coughed. "I'm sorry I didn't find that, Sir Burton," he said. "I can't say it would make much difference, though."

"Surely it makes an immense difference!" protested Mrs. Roosevelt.

"It's a big step, ma'am," said Kennelly, "from finding the apartment was broken into to deciding the burglar poisoned the bitters."

"Quite," agreed Sir Alan. "I'll replace the lock now."

As Sir Alan worked at the door, Mrs. Roosevelt stood outside and surveyed the hallway of the apartment building. There were four apartments on the floor, designated *A, B, C,* and *D* by corroded brass letters screwed to the doors. The hall was lighted by a single bulb. Pamela's apartment was on the second floor of the three-story building. The building was clean and uncluttered, and the hallways had been painted within the past two or three years. The place seemed to be clinging to respectability, so far successfully but with a precarious hold.

Inside again, Captain Kennelly asked Sir Alan and Mrs. Roosevelt if they were satisfied, if there was anything more they wanted to see. When they were ready to leave, he would place a new police seal on the door.

"I do have a small matter in mind," said Sir Alan.

"And what is that?"

The Scotland Yard inspector knelt before the couch in the living room. "I noticed this," he said, plucking a fragment of dark gray fabric off the upholstery. "Odd, don't you think?"

"In what way odd?" asked Mrs. Roosevelt.

"You will notice that the upholstery here is nubby," said Sir Alan. "If you were to rub a wool sweater across it, you would leave behind a substantial quantity of wool fibers. This bit of wool, though, is not from a sweater. Look at it."

The tattered, irregular fragment of wool he held on his palm was about the size of a postage stamp. It was woven wool, a tiny patch torn from something larger. It had clung to the rough upholstery of the couch and had been almost invisible because of the similarity of colors.

"Since this was found only a foot above the floor, I suppose it is a piece torn from a pair of trousers or a skirt," said Sir Alan. "More likely, I should think, a pair of trousers. Someone has sat here with torn pants, in other words."

"What's odd about that?" asked Captain Kennelly.

"Maybe nothing," said Sir Alan. "But let's speculate a bit. It is unlikely, I think, that this bit of fabric attached itself to the upholstery of the couch long before Mr. Garber was killed and Miss Rush-Hodgeborne was taken to jail. Obviously this sofa was the principal place for sitting in this room, and a little piece of cloth like that would be knocked off by someone's leg fairly soon, I should think, if the couch were in daily use."

"Still, what's odd?" asked Kennelly.

"Wool," said Sir Alan. "None of us is wearing it. Whom have you seen wearing it today? Or yesterday?" He shook his head. "Not in Washington, not in high summer. Indeed, I found myself most uncomfortable on my arrival—until I donned my tropicals."

"Well, it is odd then," said Kennelly. "What's it signify, Sir Burton?"

"I haven't the faintest notion," said Sir Alan.

"From the man who picked the lock!" exclaimed Mrs. Roosevelt. "He climbed in a window in the hallway and tore his pants and . . ."

"A prodigious leap in logic, I'm afraid," said Sir Alan. "I would like to think you are right, Mrs. Roosevelt, but you *have* leaped a wide chasm."

"It is becoming quite apparent, Captain Kennelly, that there is more to this case than has so far met the eye. Isn't it enough to slow down the rush to indict poor Pamela for murder? Indeed, isn't it time to arrange for her release on bail? It distresses me to think of her locked up in that horrible cell."

"Unfortunately for her, ma'am," said Captain Kennelly, "a few scratches inside a lock and a piece of torn wool don't overcome the evidence against her. Let's don't forget, there's still the motive, the stolen gems and all that. We *did*, you remember, find a stolen diamond in her watch."

"In her *watch!*" exclaimed Sir Alan. "Haw!"

"Didn't you know?" asked the First Lady.

"Indeed, yes, now that I think of it," said Sir Alan. "I had for a moment forgotten that circumstance."

"Anyway," said Mrs. Roosevelt, "obviously the facts are not all in place in this matter. There should be no hurry, therefore, to indict Pamela and bring her to trial. The processes of justice should halt until the investigation is *complete.*"

"How much time typically elapses in this country between arresting a murderer and hanging that murderer?" asked Sir Alan.

Captain Kennelly shrugged. "Oh," he said, "three or four months. The processes of justice have slowed down in recent years."

"So we have time then," said Sir Alan.

"Plenty of time," said Captain Kennelly. "There is time, I think, to send that bit of fabric to the F.B.I. labs for analysis and identification."

"No," said Mrs. Roosevelt firmly. "I don't want Director Hoover to know anything of what we have discovered."

Kennelly smiled. "Good," he said. "Neither do I."

"I believe," said Mrs. Roosevelt, "that I can locate a specialist who can examine this piece of wool for us. If you don't mind."

"Please do," said the captain. "I'll have one of my men take a look at Philip Garber's wardrobe, to see if he had any pants made of that kind of wool."

"You can see in her closet that she had no skirts of the kind," said Mrs. Roosevelt.

"I had noticed that, ma'am."

"Cynthia has answered questions for the F.B.I. as well as for the Washin'ton police," said Robert Dawes. "I should have thought 't would have been enough."

"Quite so, Mr. Dawes," said Sir Alan Burton. "Quite so. I should imagine the entire matter has become tiresome for you and your daughter."

Mrs. Roosevelt sat in a comfortable Queen Anne wing chair in the bedroom of Sir Alan's Mayflower Hotel suite, sipping tea and listening to the conversation through a small speaker in a box on the table beside her. She was unhappy with this procedure—that is, with eavesdropping on a conversation among others, only one of whom knew she could hear—but she told herself she was doing it for Pamela, which made it easier. It *was* marvelous to hear the conversation with such clarity. She had not supposed a hidden microphone could pick up speech this well. Certainly every microphone into which *she* had ever spoken was too big to hide in the vase of flowers where this one was concealed, and she counted Sir Alan Burton something of an electrical genius to have contrived so clever a device in his suite.

"More than tiresome, Sir Alan," said Cynthia. "It's *distressin'*. It's unsettlin' t' learn that a young man you have cared for has been *murdered.* But to be questioned by the F.B.I.—and now by Scotland Yard. . . . Well, it's an ordeal, Sir Alan. It's an ordeal."

Mrs. Roosevelt had not heard Cynthia's voice before. The young woman spoke with the accent of the border states, not of the deep South, in a voice pitched artificially high; and, as her father did, she spoke slowly and enunciated her words with emphasis and precision. The voice and accent were inconsistent with the image Mrs. Roosevelt had gained while watching her at the gambling table.

"I am extremely grateful to you both for agreeing to come here," said Sir Alan. "And let's do say that you are not being questioned, Miss Dawes. I should rather say that you have agreed to meet with me and discuss the matter of Philip Garber. You are, of course, entirely at liberty to refuse to answer anything, or indeed to get up and walk out of the hotel at any time. This is an entirely unofficial inquiry, and your father will advise you that I am utterly without authority in the States. I am only seeking your cooperation in clearing up some points that are of concern to my government."

"Very well, then," said Cynthia.

"Our interest," Sir Alan continued, "is in the theft of more than five hundred thousand pounds' worth of precious stones from the country home of the Earl of Crittenden, which—we have reason to believe—may have been participated in by Philip Garber."

"My daughter," said Dawes firmly, "would know nothin' about that."

"I am entirely certain that is so, Mr. Dawes," said Sir Alan. "She may, however, be in possession of facts which, while entirely innocent to her, could assist us in solving that crime."

"Like what?" asked Dawes.

"We are very curious to know," continued Sir Alan, "how much money young Garber had to spend. We know how much he earned. We know he spent a great deal more than that. We are interested in knowing how he came by the money."

"My daughter wouldn't know about that," said Dawes.

"Do you mind if I ask her?"

"Well . . ."

"Miss Dawes," said Sir Alan. "The New Club is a gambling club.

Did Philip Garber, to your knowledge, gamble at other clubs besides?"

"Yes. He loved to play—blackjack, chemin de fer, poker, craps. . . . He gambled at several other clubs."

"Did he win?"

"Sometimes he did."

"But on the whole?"

"On the whole, he lost a great deal of money, Sir Alan."

"Ah. And where did he come by it? Do you know?"

"Not for sure. No."

"Did he borrow money from you?" asked Dawes.

"Yes," said Cynthia quietly. "But he paid it back. When he died, he owed me five hundred dollars. He had paid back everythin' else."

"In other words," suggested Sir Alan, "he came into possession of sums of money from time to time."

"I s'pose he did," said Cynthia.

"How much did you loan him?" her father demanded.

"Well, he owed me five thousand at one time," she admitted.

"Five—!" Dawes exploded. *"You—"*

"He repaid," she said.

"You supposed you and he might marry, did you not?" asked Sir Alan.

"That's why I lent him money," she said.

Mrs. Roosevelt heard the sadness and the plea in the girl's voice, and she winced.

"Did you lend it all at once?" asked Sir Alan.

"Oh, no," said Cynthia. "I lent him a thousand one time, the first time, and he paid that back. Then I let him have a couple of thousand another time, and he paid that back, and after that it went on."

"You only knew him a few months," said Sir Alan. "In that time . . ."

"In that time, I lent him and he paid back maybe ten or twelve thousand."

"Borrowed when he lost, paid back when he won," said Dawes.

"Possibly," said Sir Alan.

"You have another possibility in mind?"

"Yes, that he repaid what he had borrowed immediately after he had sold one or more stolen gems."

"I think his daddy gave him the money," said Cynthia.

"Ah, yes," said Sir Alan. "Congressman Garber arranged to meet you a few days ago, Miss Dawes. Would it be an intrusion to ask why?"

"Yes, it would," she said.

"Tell him, Cynthia," said Dawes angrily. "Tell him what that N' Jersey ward heeler wanted."

"He wanted to know if I was carryin' a baby by Philip," said Cynthia sullenly.

"And you are not?"

"No. I'm not."

"Did Philip Garber ever actually propose marriage?"

"Yes, he did."

"And did you accept?"

"I did."

"Did he, then, give you an engagement ring, Miss Dawes?"

"No, he . . ."

"He what?" her father demanded.

"Nothin'. It doesn't make no difference."

"It makes a difference!" Dawes snapped. "He gave you what you showed your mother! And, by God, he did steal it! You gotta give it back!"

"He didn't! I can't! He—"

"You gotta!"

"Please," said Sir Alan. "What did Philip give you, Miss Dawes?"

"A goddam diamond!" shouted Dawes. "I understand it all now."

"Please, Mr. Dawes," said Sir Alan. "Now, Miss Dawes, what did Philip give you?"

"A diamond," she said tearfully. (She pronounced it "daa-mond.") "A beautiful big emerald-cut diamond. It was unset, and he said we would go to a jeweler and have it set in a ring. He said it had been his grandmother's."

"You gotta give it t' this man!" shouted Dawes.

"I don't have it!" she shrieked. "He took it back!"

Mrs. Roosevelt believed for a moment that the loud voices had somehow interrupted the electrical connection between the two rooms. Then she realized that everyone had fallen silent, doubtless while Dawes and maybe Sir Alan tried to comfort Cynthia. Listening carefully, she could hear shuffling, whispers, sobs. She sighed. She did not want to feel sympathy for Cynthia Dawes; she would rather think that Cynthia, not Pamela, had poisoned Philip Garber; but it was easy to conclude that Philip had abused the trust of both these young women and that both deserved sympathy and help.

"I suppose," said the quiet, authoritative voice of Sir Alan Burton, "that this emerald-cut diamond—and the fact that he took it back—was the origin of the violent quarrel you had with Philip Garber at The New Club about a week before he died."

"What's this?" asked Dawes. He was subdued, from the sound of him. "What big quarrel?"

"We had a fight, Daddy," said Cynthia softly. "It was loud and unladylike. I threw a bottle at him."

"How come?" demanded Dawes.

She sighed loudly. "He told me that night he'd lost a lot of money gamblin' at a club in Maryland, where they wouldn't let him owe for more than a day or two. He wanted ten thousand dollars. I said I couldn't let him have that much. Then he said he had to have my diamond back, had to sell it to raise the money to pay what he owed. I told him I wouldn't give it back. Then he said they'd hurt him, maybe even kill him, if he didn't pay. I cried over it, but I gave him the diamond back. Then he said he had to have 'a few thousand' besides. That's what he said—he had to have 'a few thousand.' I called him a fool for gamblin' as much as he did—and losin' as much as he did—and he got mad and told me I didn't know nothin'. He got to talkin' big, said he won and lost more money in a year than our family was worth—talk like that. I got mad. He got mad. We had an awful fight."

"You told me," said Dawes, "that he asked you to spend the night with him in another girl's apartment in Washin'ton. You said that was what he did that upset you."

"He did that too," she said. "He gave me the key to that other girl's apartment. In fact, I did spend a night with him there, Daddy. I thought we were in love and were gonna get married. He said this other girl was just a friend now, though she'd been his girlfriend in the past."

"Do you know who that former girlfriend was?" asked Sir Alan.

"Yes," said Cynthia somberly. "It was the one who killed him—Pamela Rush-whatever. I spent a night in the apartment where he died! I've been worried the police would find my fingerprints on somethin' in there. It was a squalid little flat, Daddy. That poor girl who killed him, she didn't live well."

"Can you give me the name of the place in Maryland where he owed money?" asked Sir Alan.

"No. I can tell you some other clubs where he went."

From a window in Sir Alan's fourth-floor suite, he and Mrs. Roosevelt watched Dawes and his daughter cross the street and walk toward their car. Cynthia stopped on the walk to light a cigarette. She was engaged in earnest conversation with her father. Her face was angry, her gestures animated. She dragged deeply on the cigarette once it was lighted. The hardness that was absent from her voice was pronounced on her face.

"I wonder what she and Frank Garber really talked about," said Mrs. Roosevelt.

"So do I," said Sir Alan.

9

The First Lady, wearing a thin, rose-colored, ankle-length dress,
removed her white straw hat and sat down at her writing table.
Congressman Frank Garber took an armchair facing her.

"I am sorry to have kept you waiting, Congressman," she said. "You
know how difficult it is to keep appointments."

"That is quite all right, Mrs. Roosevelt," he said. "I have only been
waiting five minutes."

"Well, then," she said with a smile, inclining her head toward him.

"I want to tell you, Mrs. Roosevelt," he said, "that I appreciate your
interest in the death of my son and the trouble you're taking to look
into it."

"You have my deepest sympathy, of course," she said.

"Thank you."

His head was big and solid. He was bald, and his graying brown hair
was thin even along the sides. He had a large, wide mouth, with big,
strong teeth, which showed when he spoke. His eyebrows slanted
upward and peaked where they almost met above the bridge of his
nose, giving his face a look of openness and intensity. He was wearing
a wrinkled blue-and-white seersucker suit, which hung loosely from
his broad shoulders.

"You do of course understand that my interest in your son's death is
focused chiefly on establishing that Pamela Rush-Hodgeborne did
not murder him," Mrs. Roosevelt cautioned.

"Our interests coincide, Mrs. Roosevelt," said Garber. "I don't
believe that poor little English girl poisoned Phil, either. I'd be very
glad to see you prove she didn't."

Mrs. Roosevelt managed to conceal her surprise. She covered it with a warm smile. "Oh, it is good to hear you say that, Congressman," she said. "I am myself absolutely convinced Pamela did not do it."

"I hope you have found evidence to that effect," said Garber.

So that was what he wanted—to know what she had learned. "Nothing conclusive," she said blandly.

"I have given the matter a great deal of thought and made a few inquiries of my own," he said. "The difficult problem for me is trying to imagine why anyone would *want* to kill Phil. He was a headstrong boy, as you might say, and caused me a good deal of worry, but he was a good boy, basically. Naturally I am annoyed by the implication that he had something to do with the jewel theft at the estate where he worked in England. It's a typical English trick, as I see it—they can't figure out who stole the jewels, so they blame it on the American who happened to be in the house."

"Pamela says he had nothing to do with it," said Mrs. Roosevelt.

"She does? Well, that's something. She was there. She should know."

"Yes."

The congressman crossed his legs. "Have you come up with any motive?" he asked. "Any other suspects?"

"I have heard," said Mrs. Roosevelt, "that Philip owed a lot of money to some unsavory people who run gambling clubs."

"I know about that," said Garber.

"A few names have been mentioned," she said. "The most interesting of them seems to be a man called Gully Balzac."

"Never heard of him," said the congressman.

"Neither had I," said she.

"I paid off a few gambling debts for him from time to time. Amounted to a hundred dollars—maybe two hundred—over the years."

Mrs. Roosevelt nodded. "I see."

The congressman frowned and licked his lips. "What is your impression—if you don't mind my asking—of that girl over in Falls Church? Cynthia Dawes?"

"I haven't met her," said Mrs. Roosevelt, "though I've heard a bit about her."

"She thought Phil was going to marry her," said Garber, still frowning. "Got very upset when she found out he wasn't. She found out, in fact, he was more interested in marrying the English girl—that is, if he was going to marry anybody: Phil was a fun-loving fellow who enjoyed his bachelorhood, if you know what I mean."

"My sons enjoyed theirs," said Mrs. Roosevelt innocently.

"Does it seem to you there's any possibility this Dawes girl killed my son? If you think about it, it would have been the perfect crime for her—doing in Phil and making it look like the girl he was most interested in had done it."

"You have met Cynthia Dawes, have you not?" asked Mrs. Roosevelt.

"Yes. After she and Phil had their tiff and stopped seeing each other, she wrote me a note and said Phil had borrowed some money from her and she wanted me to pay it. I didn't think anything of it and had no intention of paying it—until he died, and then I went out to Virginia and met her and paid her."

"What impression did she make on you?"

"Southern belle. You know the type. Smokes heavily. Drinks. I was surprised at how she drinks. Bats her eyes and talks about how innocent she is. But she's *hard*, Mrs. Roosevelt. She wanted her money. It was only fifty dollars he'd borrowed from her one night when they were out having a big time and he'd run short of cash to pay the checks, but she wanted it and took it—only a few days after my boy was murdered. She said she was sorry about him, but I wasn't sure."

"Do you really suspect her? Have you told the police you do?"

"Well . . . yes. I suspect her. But I don't have any evidence, and I haven't spoken to the police. I was wondering if you'd learned anything that might indicate she did it?"

Mrs. Roosevelt shook her head. "I've entertained the same thoughts you have, but I have seen nothing that would tend to prove she had anything to do with it."

"Well, as I said, Mrs. Roosevelt, our interests coincide. I'll be entirely honest with you. If that poor little English girl is convicted of murdering Phil, it will always be supposed the two of them had something to do with that jewel theft. I don't want that to happen. I want my son remembered as a good, honest American boy. That means a great deal to me."

"I shall remember what you've said, Congressman Garber."

The President and First Lady took lunch together, off trays on his desk in the Oval Office. The President sat behind his desk in his shirtsleeves, with the sleeves rolled back, eating sparingly, smoking, sipping coffee. Mrs. Roosevelt sat stiffly erect on her chair and nibbled on an apple.

"What an about-face!" she said. "First Garber is certain Pamela killed his son and he sets Mr. Hoover on her, then he complains to you that I am meddling in the case, and now he thanks me for the same meddling and says he hopes Pamela is innocent."

"Something very important could lie in the explanation for that," said the President.

"I think I know what, too," said Mrs. Roosevelt. "He knows about the emerald-cut diamond. He talked to Cynthia Dawes and found out about the valuable diamond Philip gave the girl and then took back from her. He knows his son had in his possession a diamond stolen from Austin House."

"Could he have helped his son smuggle the stones into the United States, or maybe helped him fence them?" asked the President. He was tired, and it was apparent that his mind was not really focused on the "Pamela problem."

"I would rather think," said Mrs. Roosevelt, "that Frank Garber is concerned about his political career. What will happen to his ambitions if it is proved that his son stole millions of dollars' worth of jewels in England, smuggled some of them into the United States, fenced them, and used the proceeds to pay gambling debts?"

The President smiled wryly. "That New Jersey district of his would re-elect Frank Garber if he stole the Washington Monument."

"Frank Garber," said Mrs. Roosevelt, "has higher ambitions than simply to be one of four hundred and thirty-five representatives to Congress."

"I wonder if he's called off everybody's favorite gumshoe," the President mused.

"Director Hoover?"

"Yes. He used his influence as a member of the House Appropriations Committee to send Edgar out looking for the evidence that would hang Pamela. Edgar would try to recrucify Christ for an extra hundred thousand in the F.B.I. appropriation."

"Now he'll have turned him on Cynthia Dawes, I should imagine," said Mrs. Roosevelt. "Poor girl."

"Yes," said the President grimly, wearily. "There will be pressure on the girl to keep quiet."

Mrs. Roosevelt dreaded her visits to the jail, but she regarded it as a duty to go and see Pamela from time to time—knowing the girl received no other visitors. She was escorted into the cell block each time, to avoid being seen by the crowds of people in the visitors' area, and each time she found Pamela wan and despondent. Now enduring the tenth day in her tiny cell, Pamela admitted that she had lost hope and expected to be put to death in the electric chair.

"I am told," she said quietly through the bars, "that one's head is shaved and that one is led into the execution chamber quite naked."

"Oh, no, my child!" protested Mrs. Roosevelt. "No such thing!"

"Well, that's what they say. The others in here seem to have some knowledge of all such things, and that is what they tell me."

"They are lying to you, Pamela," said Mrs. Roosevelt. "They are making cruel jokes."

Pamela sighed. "Anyway, they say the matter is quite swift and entirely painless—much preferable to being hanged, as I would suffer in England."

Mrs. Roosevelt shook her head. "Tell me, Pamela," she said, "how often did Philip have access to your watch?"

Pamela blushed. "You are asking me how often he spent the night in my room—or later in my flat," she protested. "It was often—whenever he wished."

"I want you to try to remember something, Pamela," said Mrs. Roosevelt. "Did Philip ever wear a dark gray wool suit in your apartment?"

Pamela shook her head. "Never. I don't think he owned such a suit."

"Do you own a dark gray wool skirt?"

"No."

"We found a bit of dark gray fabric—torn from a pair of trousers or a skirt, perhaps—clinging to the upholstery of your sofa. Do you have any idea where it came from?"

"No, Mrs. Roosevelt. I have no idea."

"It may be important, Pamela."

"I am sorry. I have no idea."

Mrs. Roosevelt smiled. "Don't be sorry. That may be good news."

"I am astounded," she said that evening. "I am, I guess, an old-fashioned person, and naïve, but I had utterly no idea that such places existed."

She sat between Sir Alan Burton and Captain Edward Kennelly at a table to the side and to the rear in the almost dark main room of the Kit Kat Club in Maryland. It was almost ten o'clock. She had wrapped her hair in a turban, was wearing big dark glasses, and held in her mouth a short amber holder with an unlighted cigarette. The cigarette and the hand she held to it most of the time served to disguise her mouth and chin, which were so characteristic a part of her and would have led, more than anything else, to her recognition. She had viewed herself in the mirror for some time before she left the White House, and had assured herself that what Sir Alan and Captain Kennelly said was true—that she would not be recognized on this foray into the dimly lighted precincts of the Kit Kat Club. ("Indeed, ma'am, I wouldn't take the responsibility if I thought there was any chance," Kennelly had said. And Sir Alan had eyed her skeptically and pronounced her "indistinguishable from Miss Greta Garbo.") Anyway, Kennelly had told her, it was not rare for people to go "slumming" in the Kit Kat Club—and so it was not unusual to come incognito.

At the door, Captain Kennelly—the only one of them who spoke the kind of English the club doorkeeper expected to hear—said he was Bill Jenkins and he was bringing Mr. and Mrs. Douglas Foraker to the club as his guests. He said Peter McIntosh of The New Club had called Gully and said it was okay to let them in. McIntosh had indeed called. That had been arranged. They were admitted into the Kit Kat as slumming Virginians and led to a table.

At a few tables around the rear and sides of the room, people sat and drank. In the center, others played at gambling tables—blackjack, roulette, craps, keno. At the far end of the room, a trio of black musicians played jazz, and on a small stage behind them a blonde had just begun to dance. The air of the room was so heavy with tobacco

smoke that the musicians and the stage were only dimly seen from
Kennelly's table.

"Can one—obtain a cup of coffee?" asked Mrs. Roosevelt uneasily,
as she glanced around and saw that people at the other tables were
drinking.

"Better order whiskey," said Kennelly. "You don't have to drink
it."

Mrs. Roosevelt squinted through the blue smoke and focused on
the blonde dancing on the stage. The girl was slowly unfastening a
pink satin dress. The First Lady nudged Sir Alan and whispered, "I
think we're about to see a striptease!"

"Oh. . . . Well, we don't have to watch," said Sir Alan, turning his
eyes away.

"I, for one, intend to watch closely," said Mrs. Roosevelt. "In the
circumstances, I may as well learn what it is like."

Her attention was distracted by a burly waiter, to whom Captain
Kennelly gave an order for three whiskies. "And tell Gully that Bill
Jenkins is here and would like to see him," he added.

Mrs. Roosevelt looked at the gamblers at the tables. She saw no one
she recognized except Martin Dies, chairman of the House Un-
American Activities Committee, conspicuously drunk and slouched
over a blackjack table. She looked at the stage again. The girl had
removed her skirt and was dancing bare-legged in a loosened pink
satin jacket and an odd garment, also of pink satin, that looked something like an Indian's breechclout, worn around her hips, exposing
them and her belly and navel. As she danced, she shook and swung
the broad strips of satin that hung to her knees in front and rear. Men
at the nearby tables had begun to applaud, and some of them made
raucous comments.

The waiter was quick to bring their drinks—six of them, not three,
commenting that there was a two-drink minimum. Except for the
necessity of maintaining her incognito, Mrs. Roosevelt would have
protested. She tasted the whiskey. It was raw, strong. She sipped
water and put the little whiskey glass aside. Captain Kennelly
drained his shot glass at a gulp, put it down before her, and slid her
full glass across the table to himself. He winked.

"Care for a little keno, folks?" the waiter returned to ask. "Got
room at the keno table."

"Gotta talk to Gully first," said Kennelly.

Sir Alan, following Captain Kennelly's lead, drained his shot glass, with a wry face, put the empty glass before Mrs. Roosevelt, and took her second glass. She sipped water and smiled.

"I hope that doesn't embarrass you," said the captain, nodding toward the stage, where the girl had now tossed aside her little jacket and was dancing in a pink satin brassière.

"Not at all," Mrs. Roosevelt said, smiling. "I *am* curious to know how far she will go."

"Our friendly host," said Captain Kennelly ominously, inclining his head toward a man approaching their table. "Gully Balzac."

Balzac was a short, beetle-browed, square-faced man—dark and scowling—dressed in a double-breasted olive-green, pinstriped suit. He frowned at them when he arrived at their table.

"Who's Jenkins?" he asked.

"Actually," said Captain Kennelly, "Pete McIntosh didn't know who he was sending to see you, Gully. I'm Captain Ed Kennelly, chief of detectives, D.C. police."

"You got no jurisdiction here," growled Balzac.

"You want to make a point of that, go ahead," said Kennelly. "I can get all the jurisdiction I need in two minutes—which you well know. Have a seat, Gully. Have a drink."

Balzac glanced at Mrs. Roosevelt and Sir Alan Burton, taking no trouble to conceal his hostility. He sat down. "What you got in mind?" he asked.

"Phil Garber owed you ten grand," said Kennelly bluntly.

"No! No," Balzac protested. "He never owed me no ten grand."

"Hell he didn't."

"Hell he did! Makes no difference, anyway. He paid."

"Ten grand," said Kennelly.

Balzac turned down the corners of his wide mouth. He shook his head. "No. He never owed ten."

Kennelly shrugged. "Whatever. Seven. Eight."

"What's the diff, anyway?" asked Balzac. "Like I said, the kid paid off, every nickel. What you got in mind, Kennelly—that I knocked the kid off by puttin' Drano in his goddam cocktail? You know better. I don't operate like that."

Mrs. Roosevelt withdrew into the shadows, as far back from the table as she could, for fear that this ugly man might recognize her. She was fascinated by him, as she had been sometimes fascinated by the venomous reptiles kept in glass-topped boxes in menageries. He was at least as repulsive.

"I know, Gully," said Kennelly. "You break their arms and legs first. Phil knew how you operate. Right?"

It was Balzac's turn to shrug.

"You muscled him, anyway," said Kennelly.

Balzac showed an ugly grin. "I explained to him he had to pay what he owed. The boy was unlucky. He dropped a lot of dough at the tables."

"He come here alone?" asked Kennelly.

"Sometimes. Sometimes with a broad."

"Who?"

Balzac shrugged again.

"Cynthia Dawes?" asked Kennelly.

"I don't know no Cynthia Dawes."

"She knows you."

"Lotta people know me."

"Don't crap around, Gully."

"Okay, okay. He came in sometimes with the Dawes girl. So what?"

"So nothin', Gully. So nothin'. Just don't crap around. So he came in here with Cynthia Dawes and dropped a lot of dough. He owed you. Then he paid you. How'd he pay you?"

"How? He came in and paid me. What else?"

"C'mon, Gully. With what? What'd he pay you with?"

"What?" asked Balzac. "What? He paid me Uncle Sammy's green foldin' money, what else? You think I'd take a check?"

"But he offered something first," said Kennelly. "What about what he offered first?"

"Ah!" said Balzac. "I get it." He snapped his fingers at the waiter, who had hovered nearby throughout this conversation. " 'Nother round," he said. "For everybody." He smiled at Kennelly, then at Mrs. Roosevelt and Sir Alan. "I get it. Okay. But I'm no fence. I don't take nothin' but money, no matter how much you owe. I ain't interested in no hot merchandise. I don't ask where you got your dough, but you convert your merchandise to dough before you deal with Gully."

"He had good merchandise, though, didn't he?" asked Kennelly.

"I expect so," said Balzac. "Yeah. I expect he did at that. I wouldn't touch it. 'Family heirloom,' he said. I bet it was—but not from *his* family."

"He ever offer you merchandise before?" asked Kennelly.

Balzac frowned at Mrs. Roosevelt. She covered her mouth with her hand and coughed. His curiosity was growing more intense.

"Did he, Gully?" Kennelly pressed. "Other merchandise?"

Balzac exhaled. "I don't know why I talk with you, Kennelly."

"Because I can put a lot of muscle on you if you don't, that's why," said Kennelly. "And it doesn't make any difference to you, does it?"

Once more Balzac shrugged. "I got no secrets," he said.

Kennelly laughed. "Who's the girl, incidentally," he asked, nodding toward the stripper on the stage. "Is that Betty McDougal, by any chance?"

"Didn't you pay any attention to the announcement?" asked Balzac. "That's Désirée LaFlamme, from Paris." He chuckled. "Sure, she's Betty McDougal. Friend of yours?"

"Sure. Call her over when she's finished," said Kennelly.

Mrs. Roosevelt stared hard at the girl. Almost nothing of the pink satin remained on her body now—only two large round patches on her breasts and the breechclout around her hips. The girl seemed to be blushing, though Mrs. Roosevelt could not be sure if her cheeks were red from embarrassment or from the heat of the lights over her little stage.

"Anyway, the other merchandise I asked you about," said Kennelly. "Did Garber have other merchandise?"

"Yeah. The kid had other merchandise a couple of times," said Balzac. "Same kind. Where you figure he got it?"

"Like to know," said Kennelly.

The waiter put two more little shot glasses before each of them. Mrs. Roosevelt made a show of tasting the whiskey in one of hers. To her surprise, it was different whiskey. It was smoother, better. The three men each tossed off a shot.

Balzac fixed a stare on Mrs. Roosevelt. "You haven't introduced your friends, Kennelly," he said.

"Mr. and Mrs. Douglas Foraker, of Virginia," said Kennelly.

Balzac grinned and nodded. "Sure," he said. He glanced at the stripper. She had finished, and he lifted his hand and snapped his fingers. She saw him and nodded.

As Balzac's attention was on the stripper, Kennelly grabbed one of Mrs. Roosevelt's shot glasses, drank the whiskey, and thrust it into her hand. When Balzac looked to the table again, she sat with the empty glass in her hand, smiling innocently.

"Did the congressman ever pay off any of his son's markers?" Kennelly asked.

"Hey, ain't I square with you, Kennelly?" Balzac asked. "Why you want to ask me embarrassing questions? I told you too much already, just to be nice to a cop."

The stripper fastened her pink satin brassière and stepped down from the stage. She hurried through the crowd, a gauntlet of men who grabbed for her and yelled propositions. Balzac reached out with his toe and hooked an extra chair from a nearby table, and when the girl reached the table he kicked it toward her.

"Betty," he said. "This is, uh, Bill Jenkins and Mr. and Mrs. Foraker. They're friends of Phil Garber."

"Glad to meet ya," said the stripper as she accepted a glass of whiskey from Balzac.

Mrs. Roosevelt could not hide her surprise. The girl sat at their table bare-legged, with nothing covering her body but the pink satin brassière and the breechclout. Her belly and navel were exposed, as were much of her hips and all of her legs. She had a blue bruise on the pallid skin of her right leg.

"Did you know Phil Garber?" Kennelly asked the girl.

The girl tossed off her whiskey and nodded. "Used to see him around," she said. She rubbed her round little belly. "Nice fella."

"How long did you know him?" asked Kennelly.

"Oh, Phil goes way back," said the girl, her voice trailing off as she looked to Balzac for a cue.

"How long? When'd you meet him?"

The girl lifted her chin. "What're you, a cop?" she asked.

"He's a cop," said Balzac.

"Shee-it," said the girl.

" 'Nother round," said Balzac to the waiter.

"How far back?" Kennelly persisted.

"Well . . . what is it, Gully? Three years?"

Balzac nodded. "That's why I call him the kid. He was one when he rst came in."

"He have money to lose then?" Kennelly asked.

"A little. He was always well fixed."

"He have merchandise?"

"Well . . ."

"Which means yes," said Kennelly. "Did his father know he had merchandise?"

Balzac shook his head. "I don't think so. Look, how would I know? But I don't think so."

The others were drinking their whiskey. Mrs. Roosevelt lifted her lass tentatively, watched her chance, and, when neither Balzac nor he girl could see, tossed the liquor on the floor. Sir Alan could not uppress a grin as she smiled ingenuously at Balzac and raised her vater glass and mimed taking a chaser.

"In other words," said Kennelly, "the boy always had merchanise."

"He always had money," said Balzac.

"Especially since he got back from England," said Kennelly.

Balzac nodded.

The waiter was quick. He put two more glasses of whiskey in front f each of them. Sir Alan looked at his with alarm. Kennelly frowned. Mrs. Roosevelt smiled. The stripper gulped hers hungrily.

Kennelly smiled at the girl. "Let's see, Betty. You've done a couple f stretches in the joint, haven't you? A year in Delaware, six months n the D.C. jail. What was that for?"

The girl stiffened and settled an angry stare on Kennelly. "None a er biz," she said.

"Your F.B.I. sheet says it was for receiving stolen merchandise."

The girl shrugged. "What's it say I been doin' lately?" she asked.

Kennelly smiled at Balzac. "Must be handy, having a fence on the premises."

Balzac shook his head. "Try again, Kennelly," he said. "If I had omethin' to fence, I wouldn't do it with a stupid broad that got erself caught twice in two years with hot merchandise in her room.

You're on the wrong track. Nowadays Betty makes her living takin off her clothes in public."

Kennelly looked back to the girl. "Did you ever do any busines with Phil Garber?" he asked.

Balzac interrupted before the girl could answer. "Better tell hin the truth, Betty," he said.

The stripper frowned. "No, not really," she said tentatively. "He showed me some stuff once. I had a contact, but I didn't know Phi very well then, and I was afraid to touch it."

"What'd he have?" Kennelly demanded.

"A necklace. Coupla rings. It was hot merchandise, but don't ask me where he got it. He didn't tell me, and I didn't ask."

"When was this, Betty?"

"It was between the time I did in Delaware and the time I did in the D.C. jail. That makes it about a year and a half ago. Yeah, a year and a half—about."

Not much later they left the Kit Kat. Gully Balzac walked to the parking lot with them. Both Captain Kennelly and Sir Alan Burton were visibly wobbly from the whiskey they had drunk.

"Well, Mrs. uh, *Foraker,*" said Balzac, with a grin and a wink. " didn't vote for your husband either time, but if I'd known he had a lady who can hold liquor like you, I just might have. Maybe you and him are real folks."

10

It was difficult to focus her attention on anything else when so many suggestive clues claimed her attention, when also her feelings of sympathy and urgency were so strong; but she was the First Lady, with responsibilities of her own making as well as those of the position, and for a whole day she had to give herself to things other than the problem of Pamela Rush-Hodgeborne.

In the morning the column had to be written—the writing crammed into the intervals between appointments with a delegation from a social agency for the redemption of wayward girls in Chicago, a committee of university teachers against fascism, and the representatives of a foundation raising money to fund Danish-American cultural exchanges. Her secretary, Tommy Thompson, was back from a short vacation, and together they looked through the morning's mail, choosing a few letters for personal response, regretfully but necessarily assigning a stock response to most. At noon she spoke to a luncheon of alumnae of Wilberforce College. When she returned to the White House, the chief usher was waiting to review with her the arrangements for the evening's reception and dinner. She finished the column, then received the wives of the Alabama Democratic Central Committee, who were in Washington for a meeting with the Alabama congressional delegation. She dressed for the reception and dinner, and promptly at seven was in the receiving line beside the President to greet an odd assortment of guests the President had invited to the White House as part of his continuing campaign to win support for his plans to support Britain and France in the event of a European war. The guests included senators, representatives, newspaper editors and reporters, several famous broadcasters, the secretary of state, and an assortment of people she could not place. She was pleased to see her daughter Anna, who was a guest for the dinner and would remain as a guest in the White House for a week, though she had little chance to talk to her that evening.

"I understand," she had said to the President during the only moment she had to speak with him—as he was taking his daily swim in the pool late in the afternoon—"that Sir Alan Burton, contrary to his reputed instructions, has begun to take a personal interest in the acquittal of Pamela."

"I think you have sold him on the idea," said the President from the water. He was without his pince-nez and squinted upward at her. "Though I am uneasy about the whole thing, frankly. I cannot understand why the Chamberlain government would send a high-powered fellow like Sir Alan Burton here . . . unless there is some larger issue involved, something they're not telling us."

"The Austin House burglary was one of the biggest jewel thefts in history. More than two million—"

"I know, Babs, I know," said the President. "But I made a quick, unofficial inquiry into the name and reputation of Sir Alan Burton. He made his name protecting state secrets, suppressing scandal, confounding plots to embarrass His Majesty's government . . . stuff like that. Second-story men are not his usual prey, no matter how much loot was taken."

"Officially, he's in Stockholm right now," said Mrs. Roosevelt.

"Officially, he's at home in London, minding the store," said the President. "*Unofficially,* he's in Stockholm, which is where my confidential source thinks he is. So I suppose it must be *ununofficially* that we find him here. Anyway, no one in London has *officially* heard from him for six weeks. Too many levels of secrecy for me. That's what makes me think there's more to his being here than he's telling us."

"Still, we are fortunate that he's here. Don't you think?"

The President swam across the pool and back, moving athletically with strong strokes of his muscled arms. Returning to her edge of the pool, he tossed the water off his face by throwing his head back. "Be careful of Frank Garber," he said. "He is treacherous."

"I don't believe a word he says."

"That's a good policy."

"If Philip stole the earl's jewels—as I am now convinced he did—it was not the first time he was involved in such a theft. He was a thief before he went to England."

"That doesn't save Pamela, though," said the President. "What evidence do you have to prove she did not poison his drink?"

"*Worlds* of suggestive facts," said Mrs. Roosevelt. "Nothing that proves anything."

"Who, in heaven's name, is *that?*" she whispered to the President as they stood in the receiving line and a tall, gawky, dark-haired man —his head dominated by his outsized ears—approached.

"That's Sam Rayburn's protégé, a Texas congressman called Johnson," said the President. "Ambitious young fellow. Never mind him. Want to see something pretty, look at his wife."

The congressman from Texas shook her hand and spoke with the practiced intense sincerity of the professional politician, and Mrs. Roosevelt smiled back with equally practiced warmth. The congressman introduced his wife as "Lady Bird," and the name alone, as much as the President's recommendation, won Mrs. Roosevelt's interest. She told Mrs. Johnson she was pleased to meet her and asked her to come to the White House for tea on Wednesday.

"Another Texan," the President whispered to her a few minutes later. "Texas is famous for oil and snakes, and here comes both of them personified."

He spoke of Martin Dies, who approached in the line, filled with the self-confidence, the arrogance, that characterized his continuing performance as the feared, flamboyant chairman of the House Committee on Un-American Activities.

"Ah, Mr. Dies," she said. "I can pass along the best wishes of a good friend of yours."

"Indeed, ma'am," Dies said, smiling. "And who might that be?"

"Mr. Balzac," she said, with a nod and a wicked smile.

Dies blanched. "I, uh, don't recall anyone by that name," he said cautiously.

"Mr. Gulliver Balzac," she said with mock innocence. "At least I assume his name is Gulliver. Gully. Gully Balzac."

Dies drew in his breath. "Uh, no, ma'am. I sincerely don't know anyone by that name."

"And Miss LaFlamme. She speaks very highly of you, Mr. Dies."

"Uh . . . It's very nice to see you, Mrs. Roosevelt," said Dies, and he moved quickly on down the line.

The President leaned his head toward her and whispered, "What'd you do to him?"

She smiled. "Just amusing myself a little," she said lightly.

Sir Alan Burton came to the White House the next morning. She met him in the President's oval study on the second floor, since her own office was being cleaned. There, in the midst of the President's famous collection of naval prints, they sat and took coffee.

"Something interesting, if I may say so," said the sandy-haired Englishman. "That bit of fabric we found in Miss Rush-Hodgeborne's flat . . . you recall?"

"I do, of course."

"It was sent where you suggested, to the Naval Intelligence Laboratory. Because of your call, they agreed to examine and test it. It has been returned now to Captain Kennelly, but the laboratory report is interesting."

"And it says?"

"It's a very complete report, the kind of thing my own labs at the Yard would do. I have a lot of respect for the men who did it. They say the bit of fabric is wool, as we supposed. They believe it is from a garment that has been worn for some time. They deduced that from the amount of dust and other foreign material their microscopic examination found embedded in the weave. What is more, they performed a chemical analysis of the dye used to color the wool. It is a dye used in Scotland. It is not employed in this country, so far as they know. They conclude that the garment from which the bit of fabric was torn was tailored from a Scottish woolen. That means it was an expensive pair of trousers."

"An expensive wool suit," Mrs. Roosevelt mused. "Being worn in Washington in the summer. It suggests . . ."

"Yes?"

"It suggests the man who broke into Pamela's apartment was a visitor who didn't know how inappropriate his suit would be in this city at this time of year."

"Perhaps," said Sir Alan.

"A visitor from England, do you suppose?"

"Perhaps."

"So all we have to do is look for an Englishman with torn pants," he said.

"Captain Kennelly has detailed men to inquire of the tailors' shops in the city," said Sir Alan. "If he engaged a tailor to have his trousers repaired . . ."

"Then we would have him!" she said with enthusiasm.

"Indeed we would," agreed Sir Alan. "But whom would we have, I wonder?"

"A man who broke into Pamela's apartment and put poison in her bottle of bitters."

Sir Alan smiled. "I wish it were that simple. That is a guess. Even if we find the man, we will have no evidence that he put the potassium cyanide in the bitters."

"That evidence," she said with confidence, "will be found when we know who the man is."

"Perhaps."

"Let me change the subject, Sir Alan. I've done something wicked. I have prevailed on a banker to breach a confidence. It has been worthwhile, however. I've learned something interesting."

"And what is that?"

"Three days before the death of Philip Garber, Cynthia Dawes withdrew four thousand dollars from a savings account in a Virginia bank."

"Ah," said Sir Alan. "That is a suggestive fact, I suppose—though I cannot say I am sure what it suggests."

"I cannot either," she said. "It is even more suggestive, though, that she demanded twenty-dollar bills. Two hundred of them. What do you suppose she did with two hundred twenty-dollar bills?"

"Paid some more of Garber's gambling debts, perhaps," said Sir Alan.

"Four thousand dollars," said Mrs. Roosevelt. "And Frank Garber said Philip owed her fifty dollars."

"Congressman Garber lies, I regret to say," said Sir Alan.

"I should like," said Mrs. Roosevelt, "to know what became of the emerald-cut diamond."

"I have looked into that," said Sir Alan. "One of the items in the inventory of stones taken from the earl is an emerald-cut diamond, a moderate-sized but particularly fine one, known to cognoscenti as the Raphael diamond. It is worth as much as three thousand pounds."

"More than fifteen thousand dollars," said Mrs. Roosevelt.

Sir Alan nodded. "At the current rate of exchange. I have asked Captain Kennelly to put a description of it on the international police wire, stating that it may be in the States."

"Gully Balzac lied to us about something, then," she said.

"I would suspect he lied in everything he said to us."

She smiled. "But I have one particular matter in mind. He said Philip Garber offered him 'merchandise' in payment of his gambling debt. If the merchandise was the Raphael diamond, he would not have refused to take it in payment of Philip's gambling debt. A man like that would not refuse to take a stone worth far more than the debt."

"Well, he might have," said Sir Alan.

"Why?"

"There would be a substantial risk in buying a stolen gem like that. Only a sophisticate could possibly recognize it, but there would be a risk in buying it. What is more, a fence would not give him a sum anywhere near its value."

"Why not?"

"What could anyone do with it?" asked Sir Alan. "If it were returned to the channels of commerce, sooner or later it would be recognized, traced. If it were larger, someone might cut it up into smaller stones. But the Raphael is valuable for its purity and color, not for its size, and there isn't enough of it to cut up."

"It would certainly be helpful if it were to show up," she said.

"It may never show up," said Sir Alan. "We may be on the wrong track entirely. It has occurred to me that it is inconsistent with the character of Philip Garber that he should have given so valuable a stone to Cynthia Dawes. Are we to suppose he loved the girl so much as to give her the most valuable stone from the earl's collection?"

"Is the Raphael diamond the most valuable single stone the earl lost in the burglary?"

"Yes," said Sir Alan.

"Then we may surmise that Philip took the best loot from the burglary," said Mrs. Roosevelt. "Unless he worked alone . . ."

"He didn't work alone," said Sir Alan. "We know that at least two other men took part in the burglary. Someone silenced the watch dogs, someone opened the safe. . . . We found lots of footprints."

Captain Kennelly arranged for Pamela Rush-Hodgeborne to be brought to his office, and he allowed Mrs. Roosevelt and Sir Alan Burton to talk with her alone. Wan and disconsolate, Pamela sat stiffly on a wooden chair, in a jail uniform much too small for her, self-consciously trying to pull the skirt down to her knees. The day was hot, and the small electric fan that rattled the papers on the captain's desk labored in vain.

"I *think,*" said Mrs. Roosevelt to Pamela, "that Sir Alan has come to believe in your innocence, as I do."

Pamela cast him a skeptical glance.

"Mrs. Roosevelt refers to innocence of murder," said Sir Alan. "I cannot yet dispel the suspicion that you took some part—perhaps a very minor part—in the burglary."

"Then if I do not die in the electric chair here, I shall return to England to begin serving a long term in prison," she said. "I am not sure which I would choose, had I the choice."

"Pamela," said Mrs. Roosevelt. "Did you know that Philip brought another girl to your apartment while you were in New York with me? Did you know she spent the night with him there?"

"Oh!" said Pamela, suddenly regaining color, suddenly angry. "That explains—" She stopped, drew a breath. "She was a thief!"

"A thief?"

"Yes," said Pamela. She sighed. "Though what difference does it make now?"

"Who knows what difference?" said Sir Alan. "Tell us about this theft."

Pamela sighed again. "In London—oh, almost a year ago—I bought a lovely jar of lavender-scented cream. A big jar, it was, and I used it sparingly, because it was so expensive. It had been an indulgence, you see. I know I hadn't used half of it, but I kept it in my bathroom and put a bit of it on my face from time to time. It did smell so lovely.

. . . When I returned from New York, the jar was missing. I searched everywhere for it. If he took another girl to my apartment and let her sleep in my bed and use my things—well, then. She must have liked my lavender cream as much as I did!"

Mrs. Roosevelt and Sir Alan exchanged glances. "Not Cynthia, surely," said Sir Alan.

"No," said Mrs. Roosevelt. "I think not."

"Who is Cynthia?" asked Pamela.

"The girl who spent the night in your apartment," said Mrs. Roosevelt. "But she is independently wealthy and seems an unlikely person to steal a jar of face cream."

"Then others . . ." Pamela whispered, frowning.

"Did you ever have reason to suspect that Philip brought others to your flat?" asked Sir Alan.

"Indeed not," said Pamela firmly. "This Cynthia is a surprise."

"He had a latchkey, I suppose," said Sir Alan.

"Yes."

Mrs. Roosevelt put a finger to her mouth. "I wonder what secret visitors you had, Pamela," she said. "And why."

"You might ask Alicia Howell," said Pamela.

"Who is Alicia Howell?"

"She lives in the flat above mine. She's at home during the day, and she might have heard people in my flat. Also, her dog would have barked if anyone strange were downstairs. He barked at me at first, until he got used to me—then at Philip, until he got used to him. If Philip brought in anyone who shouldn't have been there, that dog might have barked. I always felt safe from burglars there because of Alicia's dog."

"I wonder," said Mrs. Roosevelt, "if the dog barked when someone broke into your apartment and put the poison in the bitters."

"Oh, dear, let's hope so!" said Pamela. "It would be evidence, wouldn't it?"

"It would," said Sir Alan. "And I wonder if the police questioned Miss Howell about this?"

"It would be evidence against me, though, if the dog didn't," said Pamela.

"We won't mention it to Captain Kennelly," said Mrs. Roosevelt, with a small smile. "At least we won't just yet."

11

"I can't express to you," said Mrs. Roosevelt to Sir Alan Burton, "the depth of my gratitude for all the help you are giving me. I can only believe you have come to believe as fully as I do in the innocence of the poor girl."

Sir Alan's face reddened until it shone, and he frowned and cleared his throat. She sat at her breakfront desk, facing the morning's accumulation of mail, and he sat opposite her, his forehead glistening, damp with the morning heat and humidity. Mrs. Roosevelt glanced over a list he had just given her.

"I asked Sir Rodney to obtain from the Foreign Office a list of everyone who left England en route to the States during the month before the murder," he explained. "He had clerks check that list against the Yard's records, to see how many had criminal records. That's what you have in hand there—a list of every convicted or suspected felon who left England for the States in that month."

She frowned over the names: a dozen of them.

"Notice Barton there," said Sir Alan. "Murdered his wife, as we always believed, though he was acquitted of it. Curious coincidence that he should come to the States in the month before the death of Philip Garber."

"Why curious?" she asked.

"Poisoned her, as we've always believed," said Sir Alan. "At any rate, she died of poison."

"Potassium cyanide?" she asked.

He shook his head. "Strychnine, unfortunately. But look, too, at the name Bullock. That old fellow was released from Dartmoor only ten months ago. He'd served a term for burglary—the third term for

burglary he's served since 1924. Unless I'm wholly wrong, he's come
to the States to recover a part of the loot from some long-ago burglary. Damned clever burglar, Bullock. Could have been one of the
burglars at Austin House, I supose."

"Have you shown this list to Captain Kennelly?"

"I expect to, when he arrives."

"I am sure he'll be interested," she said.

"Another bad name there," said Sir Alan. "Billingham. He and
Gully Balzac would have much in common, except that Billingham's
a much worse sort. General underworld type, as you might say. He
couldn't have come to the States for any good purpose. He never
does anything for a good purpose. Long arrest record, but nothing
major has ever been proved against him."

"I wonder," said Mrs. Roosevelt, "if any of these men came to the
United States wearing dark wool suits."

Sir Alan smiled smugly. "Barton," he said, "uses a Savile Row tailor.
He inherited a great deal of money from the wife who died of poison.
Bullock is a proletarian sort, who I would not suppose ever owned a
proper suit of clothes. Billingham—well, we can't be sure of him.
We've checked the others on the list. Lockwood there is a professional gambler, which is suggestive, too. He has spent time in prison
for petty theft. Millhouse is a pimp. Dugan is a smuggler. And so on."

"Have you photographs of these men?"

"Indeed we have. They are being flown to the States. The list was
wired."

"Excellent," she said.

"I have something more," said Sir Alan. He handed her another
paper. "This is an exact description of the Raphael diamond. A photograph of that is on its way, too."

She frowned over the description. "I can't say this is very meaning-
ful to me," she said.

"It is not to me, either," said Sir Alan, "but I employed an expert to
decipher it for me. The description contains an interesting bit of
information."

"What is that?"

"The Raphael diamond could not have been smuggled out of Austin House, or into this country, in Miss Rush-Hodgeborne's lapel

watch. It is substantially too large to fit into the channel inside the watch case."

"And what does that mean?"

Sir Alan shrugged. "I don't know. But it adds a new complexity to the investigation."

"I think," said Mrs. Roosevelt, "that when Captain Kennelly arrives, we should go out to visit Miss Alicia Howell. I want to know if her dog barked."

"I am curious about that myself."

Captain Kennelly arrived some ten minutes later, confessing that he had never before seen the inside of the White House and expressing a hope that he would find the time someday soon to walk through its famous rooms. Mrs. Roosevelt suggested she show him through now, but Captain Kennelly shook his head and said something important had happened in the Garber–Rush-Hodgeborne case and that he could not take the time, much as he would like to, to tour the White House that morning.

"What?" asked Mrs. Roosevelt. "Please tell us, Captain. We—"

"The Alexandria police, over in Virginia, have found the Raphael diamond," said Kennelly. "An Alexandria jeweler telephoned my office yesterday afternoon to say he had a diamond in his shop that looked suspiciously like the Raphael. We had put the word out to be on the lookout for it, you know. He called and asked for a more complete description. I sent it over. He confirmed it last night. The diamond *is* the Raphael. The Alexandria police picked it up and are holding it."

"Who brought it into the shop?" asked Mrs. Roosevelt, almost breathless.

Kennelly smiled. "Who would you guess? Cynthia Dawes. She wanted it set in a ring."

"And she?"

"They arrested her an hour ago."

"It is *outrageous*, Mrs. Roosevelt!" Cynthia Dawes complained angrily through the steel bars of the women's dayroom at the Alexandria jail. "I've done *nothin'* wrong! Nothin'! That diamond is mine. I bought it and paid for it."

"I have nothing but sympathy for you, Miss Dawes," said Mrs. Roosevelt. "As Captain Kennelly told you, my only interest is in proving the innocence of Pamela Rush-Hodgeborne."

"T' subject a person to this kind of *humiliation* is—oh, it's *wrong*, Mrs. Roosevelt," Cynthia went on tearfully. "You're a woman with a pronounced interest in *justice*. I'm as innocent as that poor girl they accused of poisonin' Phil."

The dayroom was some fifteen feet square. The front wall consisted of a barrier of close-set heavy bars through which Cynthia protested; the remaining walls were of white-painted brick covered with pencil scribbles. Cynthia wore a green cotton dress—the jail uniform. She was barefoot.

"Why do you say Pamela is innocent?" Mrs. Roosevelt asked.

"Oh. I don't *know* she is. I just suppose they have her locked up on no better evidence of wrongdoin' than they have against me. We are both the *victims* of Phil Garber."

"The Raphael diamond, Miss Dawes," interjected Sir Alan Burton.

"I never knew the diamond had a *name* till they told me so this mornin'," said Cynthia. "Anyway, it is mine. He gave it to me, and then he took it back, and then I *bought* it."

"It will be your defense, I suppose," said Sir Alan, "that you didn't know it was stolen."

" 'Course I nevah knew it was *stolen!* He *gave* it to me! It was supposed to be the diamond in my *engagement* ring. I wouldn't have let him give me a *stolen* diamond for an engagement ring!"

"Let's put matters in sequence, Miss Dawes," said Captain Kennelly. "When did you first see the diamond?"

"When he gave it to me for an engagement ring," she insisted. "Then he took it back."

"Yes. We had an awful fight over it, but I gave it back to him."

"Then what did he do with it?"

"He *told* me he used it to pay a gamblin' debt."

"Where?"

"At th' Kit Kat Club, in Maryland."

"Gully Balzac says he didn't accept it," said Kennelly.

"That's prob'ly right," Cynthia agreed. "I'd seen Phil try to pay Gully before by handin' him diamonds, and Gully wouldn't take 'em. But the girl took it."

"What girl."

"The stripteaser."

"Betty McDougal," said Kennelly.

Cynthia nodded. She leaned against the bars. "I should never have had nothin' to do with people like that," she said quietly, sadly. "But I *swear* I didn't know the diamond was stolen. I thought he had to sell it that way because he owed and was in trouble."

"Did you buy it from Betty McDougal?"

Cynthia nodded.

"For how much?"

"Four thousand dollars."

"When and where?"

Cynthia put her forehead against one of the steel bars. When she looked up again, she had squeezed tears from her eyes, and they stood on her cheeks. "You gonna help me get out of here?" she whispered.

"Telling the truth will help you get out of here," said Kennelly sternly.

Cynthia nodded, but her eyes spoke disbelief. "Betty called me," she said. "She'd bought the diamond from Phil, and he'd handed the money over to Gully. She knew he'd given the diamond to me and knew I cared for it, so she offered to sell it back to me. She asked me five thousand dollars for it, but I said all I could get up was four. So she sold it to me for four thousand."

"How much did he owe Gully?"

"He *told* me it was ten thousand."

"What did Betty give him for the diamond?"

"Twenty-five hundred, I think."

"She's a fence," said Kennelly.

Cynthia nodded. "Phil had sold her stuff before. I think she works for somebody in Baltimore."

"When Congressman Garber came to see you, Cynthia, what did he want?" asked Mrs. Roosevelt.

"He wanted to buy the diamond," said Cynthia. "He offered me five thousand for it. I wouldn't sell. It was worth more than that—to me."

"Sentimental value?" asked Kennelly.

Cynthia nodded. "It was all I had left of Phil."

"We should, I think, in good conscience, help to arrange Cynthia's release," said Mrs. Roosevelt as she, Kennelly, and Sir Alan left the Alexandria police headquarters.

"I'll be more interested in that," said Kennelly, "when she starts telling us the truth."

"But didn't she?" asked Mrs. Roosevelt.

"Sir Burton?" asked Kennelly. "Did she, do you think?"

"I fear not," said Sir Alan. He turned and spoke to Mrs. Roosevelt as they walked toward the car. "She may not have known the diamond was the Raphael, and I'm prepared to believe she did not know specifically where it came from. She understood full well, however, that Philip Garber sold it to Betty McDougal for only a fraction of its value, and I can't believe she was so naïve she did not understand why. Then she saw an opportunity to own the diamond by purchasing it from Betty McDougal, still for only a fraction of its value. She didn't buy it for sentimental reasons. She bought it because she wanted to own an exquisite diamond and saw the chance to have one for very little money."

"She'd owned it once, and she wanted it back," said Kennelly.

"But how could she have been so naïve as to take it to a jeweler and try to have it set in a ring?" asked Mrs. Roosevelt.

"She didn't realize it was identifiable," said Sir Alan.

"She was in a better position than Betty McDougal," said Kennelly. "If Betty came to any legitimate jeweler with that diamond, it would raise an immediate suspicion. But Cynthia is known around here as a young woman of means."

"But why did Betty let her have a fifteen-thousand-dollar gem for four thousand?"

"Betty knew it was hot," said Kennelly. "She made fifteen hundred on the deal, maybe more, and was rid of a hot diamond. She was satisfied."

Mrs. Roosevelt sighed. "Very well, then. But Philip Garber surely knew the value of the diamond. Why would *he* sell it for less than twenty percent of its value?"

"He knew it was hot, too," said Kennelly. "More than the other stones taken from Austin House, it was identifiable. What's more, he was being pressed. Gully Balzac is an aggressive collector when a man owes him money."

"In the best of circumstances, he could not have gotten more than five thousand for it," said Sir Alan. "People who deal in stolen property don't pay value."

They reached the car. By now, several people on the sidewalk had recognized Mrs. Roosevelt, and she paused to smile and wave before she bent down and took her seat in the automobile.

"I believe I know," she said as they drove off, "why Frank Garber tried to buy the diamond from Cynthia."

"I should imagine you do," said Sir Alan.

"Yes," said Mrs. Roosevelt. "It stands as incontrovertible evidence that his son was indeed the Austin House burglar."

"*One* of the Austin House burglars," said Sir Alan.

"One of the Austin House burglars," she agreed. "It was perhaps the only stone that could be traced directly and absolutely, from the Earl of Crittenden to Philip to Cynthia to Betty McDougal and back to Cynthia."

"Not perhaps the only stone," said Sir Alan. "But perhaps the only one he knew about."

"In any event," said Captain Kennelly, "I think we should leave Cynthia Dawes where she is and let Virginia justice take its course. It may be they can't prove she knew the diamond was stolen, but as long as she's in jail and a bit frightened she may remember more that she would like to tell us."

"And Betty McDougal?" asked Mrs. Roosevelt.

"We've got her, too," said Kennelly. "She was in Washington early this morning. She's occupying a cell a few doors down from Pamela."

Mrs. Roosevelt shook her head unhappily. "I wish I could see how it all tends to prove Pamela's innocence."

"Think of it this way," suggested Kennelly. "It increases the number of suspects."

"Gully . . . ?" asked Mrs. Roosevelt.

"Gully, certainly," said Kennelly. "Betty McDougal. Cynthia, even."

"And someone from England," said Sir Alan. "The Raphael diamond was the most valuable stone taken from Austin House. I wonder if it was intended by the burglars that Philip Garber should have it and should bring it to the States, first to hand it over to a girlfriend, then to fence it for a sixth of its value to pay a gambling debt. If I were one of a gang of criminals who had taken an immense risk to steal a marvelous stone like that, I can't imagine I would turn it over to Philip Garber to give to a new girlfriend for her engagement ring."

"Do you suppose Philip stole from the thieves?" asked Mrs. Roosevelt.

Sir Alan frowned as he did some mental calculation. "He seems to have taken a considerable share of the loot. What with the Raphael and the other diamonds that have turned up in the States, he seems to have taken a lion's share."

Back at the White House, Mrs. Roosevelt sat down before her breakfront desk and smiled up wearily at Tommy Thompson.

"I hope it's coming along well," said Tommy. "I do feel so sorry for Pamela. I mean, a stranger in this country, and—"

"The child is a *victim*," said Mrs. Roosevelt. "I am beginning to feel that Philip Garber corrupted and victimized every young woman he knew."

"While you were out," said Tommy, "you had two messages about the Pamela business. The first is from the Countess of Crittenden. She is on her way to this country. She sailed Thursday on the *Ile de France*."

"Pamela will be grateful," said Mrs. Roosevelt.

"And Captain Kennelly called," said Tommy. "He must have called just after you left him, as soon as he reached his office and received his own messages."

"Does he want me to return his call?"

"Not necessarily. He wanted you to know that the Raphael diamond has been confiscated from the Alexandria police. Two F.B.I. agents arrived at their headquarters this afternoon and took the diamond. They told the Alexandria people that the diamond is evidence in an important federal case."

Mrs. Roosevelt's face stiffened with anger. "Oh," she said. "I see. I see all too well."

12

"The—the wife of the President of the United States!" exclaimed Alicia Howell. "Mrs. *Franklin D. Roosevelt!* Oh, I—I can't *believe* it!" She giggled nervously. "Well, do, please, make yourself comfortable, Mrs. Roosevelt. And . . . Sir Alan . . . ?"

"Burton."

"Yes, Sir Alan Burton—of Scotland Yard. Do make yourself at home, Sir Alan Burton. Uh, that chair there is, uh, a little more comfortable than this one. Uh . . . uh, tea? Would you care for tea? I can put water on. . . ."

"It really isn't necessary, Miss Howell," said Mrs. Roosevelt. "We have only come to ask you one or two questions."

"No trouble. No trouble at all. Why, I'd feel awkward if you came to my house and I couldn't at least offer you a cup of tea. And, uh, by the way, it's *Mrs.* Howell. My late husband, Captain Howell, served twenty-seven years in the United States Marine Corps."

"Mrs. Howell," said Mrs. Roosevelt, with her warmest smile. "Of course, we would be pleased to have tea with you."

"I can offer something a little stronger if you'd rather," said Alicia Howell. "A drop of whiskey?"

"Tea will be delightful," said Mrs. Roosevelt.

The woman retreated to her kitchen to put her pot of water on to heat. She had, it was apparent, already tasted the drop of whiskey she was offering, although it was early in the afternoon. Her loose-fleshed face was ravaged by whiskey and cigarettes and time. Her mascaraed eyes were all pupil, as it seemed, with hardly any iris, and she seemed not to focus; her jaw wobbled up and down like the jaw of a ventriloquist's dummy. She was dressed in an orange-and-yellow flowered crêpe wrapper, for which she had already profusely apologized. Her modest apartment was crowded with what Mrs. Roosevelt recognized now as the mementoes of her husband's long career: ivory figurines from Asia, satin pillowcases from Hawaii, brass bowls from Egypt, a tattered leopard skin from the Congo, a pair of curved steel throwing knives from Morocco, and coconuts carved as grotesque faces, with shells for eyes and bits of shell for teeth, from God knew where.

"Oh, poor Pamela," Alicia Howell said, as she returned from the kitchen and sat down. "I cannot believe—No. I *do* not believe that sweet little girl committed murder. Although . . . of course, we do know—still water runs deep, as they say. But even so, I do not believe that sweet little English girl killed the Garber boy."

"Did you know him, too?" asked Mrs. Roosevelt.

"Oh, sure. You know, Pamela lives right under me. I mean, I'm Three-C, and she's Two-C. I used to see the young man in the hallway or on the stairs. He was a good-looker! I could understand what she saw in him. Handsome! Tall—"

"Did other men come to see her?" asked Sir Alan.

Alicia Howell shook her head. "Not that I ever saw. I think she's a one-man gal. Like me."

"Did he ever bring another woman to her apartment?" asked Mrs. Roosevelt.

Alicia Howell shrugged. "Not likely."

"I'm afraid it happened, Mrs. Howell," said Mrs. Roosevelt. "We have evidence of it."

The woman's dark, unexpressive eyes hardened for a moment. "When could he have done that?"

"When Pamela was in New York with me."

Alicia Howell shook her head. "I never saw it."

"Have you been questioned much about the death of Philip Garber?" asked Mrs. Roosevelt.

"No. The cops came up that night. Then again the next day. Just for a minute each time."

"No one else?"

"No. What are you driving at, may I ask?"

Sir Alan smiled at her. "Nothing much, Mrs. Howell. You understand, we are trying to tie up a few loose ends in the case. I should be glad to hear if you heard or saw anything unusual about the time of Philip Garber's death."

Alicia Howell regarded him with a doubtful stare. "Are you on Pamela's side, or what?" she asked.

Sir Alan fumbled. "Uh . . ."

"Well, *I am,*" said Mrs. Roosevelt.

"I'd be very upset if that poor girl went to the chair," said Alicia Howell. "I won't kid you about that."

"So would I," said Mrs. Roosevelt.

Alicia Howell rose. "Let me check my tea water," she said.

While she was in the kitchen, Mrs. Roosevelt and Sir Alan glanced again around the apartment. It was exactly like the one below. It was at the rear of the building, and the view from the window was of the thin yellow grass and single small tree of a fenced backyard, shared by all the tenants in the building, apparently. Beyond the fence there was a littered alley. The monumental nature of the nation's capital was not in evidence in the view from this window.

Alicia Howell returned bearing a tray. Clear hot water steamed in three glass mugs. Beside each lay a paper tea bag. "Do you use sugar or cream in your tea?" she asked as she handed a mug and a tea bag to each of her guests.

Sir Alan regarded the tea bag and water with a horror that amused Mrs. Roosevelt. With distaste he could not conceal, he lifted his bag by its tag and lowered it on its string into the mug of steaming—not boiling—water. "Uh, a lump of sugar, if you please," he said.

Alicia Howell dumped a teaspoonful of sugar into his mug. "There," she said. "More?"

"Oh, no. Thank you."

"Nothing like a nice cup of tea, I suppose you'd say. I mean, you being English, you must love your tea. Pamela did—*does*. Myself, I favor coffee. Actually, I favor a spot of whiskey at teatime. You sure . . . ?"

"Well, p'raps a jigger."

"Ha. Mrs. Roosevelt?"

"No, thank you."

Mrs. Roosevelt smiled again when Alicia Howell returned from her kitchen bearing a pair of glasses with generous splashes of whiskey. She watched Sir Alan lift his glass to his mouth and saw his face blanch as he realized the whiskey was bourbon. He sipped manfully, though, and swallowed some tea to clear the sweetish taste of the bourbon from his mouth.

"We have a special question we want to ask you, Mrs. Howell," said Mrs. Roosevelt.

"Shoot," said Alicia Howell.

"Well, Pamela told us your dog barked whenever a stranger entered the building. We are curious about that. The night Philip Garber died, or the night before. Did your dog . . . ?"

Alicia Howell put her cup and glass aside on a table. Her face twisted into a grimace. "No," she whispered. She shook her head. She bit her lip. "Cappy—my little Cappy. I'd had him six years, Mrs. Roosevelt. Someone killed him. Someone killed Cappy the night before . . . the night before the Garber boy died downstairs."

"Oh, I am sorry," said Mrs. Roosevelt. "What happened?"

"I went out for a drink and a bite and to a movie," said Alicia Howell in a hoarse whisper. "I came back. . . . It was about nine-thirty. I came in. Cappy didn't . . . come running. He was in the kitchen. Dead. His neck was broken."

"Did you call the police?"

"Yes. They didn't care much. They said one of the neighbors must have got in and killed him to stop him barking."

"And this happened," said Sir Alan, "the very night before Philip Garber died in the apartment beneath yours? How did someone get in?"

"I don't know," said Alicia Howell sadly. "I think some of our keys fit each other's apartments. The locks ain't much, anyway."

"What kind of dog was he?" asked Sir Alan sympathetically.

Alicia Howell shrugged. "Just a dog. A mutt. He was black all over."

"Would he bite?" asked Sir Alan. "I mean, if someone broke in here, would he have bitten—or tried to?"

"Probably. Cappy could be fierce."

"Was anything stolen from your apartment that night?" asked Mrs. Roosevelt.

Alicia Howell shook her head. "No. Whoever broke in, he just broke in to hurt Cappy. I accused Mr. Drake, in the front. He always complained about Cappy. He swears he didn't, but I still suspect him.

You have to know if it had been a burglar, he would have stolen some of my things. Some of this stuff, the Captain, my husband, brought back from all parts of the world, everyplace he served. Any regular burglar would have stolen it."

"Do you mind, Mrs. Howell," asked Sir Alan Burton, "if I examine the lock on your door?"

"I agree completely," said Captain Kennelly. "It's no coincidence."

"The scratches were very much the same," said Sir Alan. "I am prepared to accept it as proved that the same burglar entered the Howell flat and the Rush-Hodgeborne flat. We did not, of course, call on the other tenants in the building and ask to disassemble their locks. I do suggest, though, that you send officers to do so."

"Two burglaries," said Mrs. Roosevelt. "Apartments Two-C and Three-C in the same building, probably the same night. Nothing stolen in either case."

"No coincidence," said Captain Kennelly.

"I should like to raise another point," said Mrs. Roosevelt.

"Of course," said Kennelly.

"Potassium cyanide," said Mrs. Roosevelt. "Where did Pamela obtain potassium cyanide? Has your investigation turned up anything to suggest where she obtained it?"

"No," said Kennelly. "Nothing."

"Then how long, Captain, will you continue to hold Pamela as a suspect in the murder of Philip Garber?"

That evening the Marine Band played on the White House lawn. The grounds were thrown open to anyone who wanted to come, and thousands did, bringing everything from elaborate picnic dinners, with champagne, in wicker hampers to bags of potato chips and bottles of beer. The President, looking relaxed and happy in a white suit, sat in a comfortable armchair, laughing and nodding in time to the music, and waving to the gabbling but respectful crowd. Mrs. Roosevelt sat beside him, smiling, chatting with people who hovered around her and the President, enjoying the hour.

Harry Hopkins sat nearby on the grass, taking an occasional sip from a glass of beer. Bernard Baruch was beside him, talking quietly.

The new young senator from Ohio, Robert Taft, the son of William Howard Taft, stood at the edge of the little group around the President, conspicuously thoughtful, perhaps remembering the days when his family had lived in the White House. General George Marshall sat on a garden bench, talking soberly with Henry Stimson, who was down from New York this week. General Marshall had introduced a spare-looking colonel named Omar Bradley, who sat on the grass talking shyly with Missy LeHand. The gawky congressman from Texas, Johnson, was there, with his wife, who had won Mrs. Roosevelt's affection. The director of the F.B.I. strolled across the lawn, resplendent in white suit and snappy white straw hat.

"She is entirely innocent, in all probability," said Hoover to the President and Mrs. Roosevelt an hour later, when they had a few minutes to talk alone. He was speaking of Pamela. "I am more inclined to believe the Dawes girl had something to do with killing Philip Garber."

"I understand you have seized the Raphael diamond," said Mrs. Roosevelt.

"It is evidence," said the director.

"Evidence of what, Edgar?" the President asked.

"I am more and more convinced there is a conspiracy to discredit Congressman Garber," said the director.

"By revealing that his son was a thief?" asked the President.

"It would be in some people's interest to have it supposed that Philip Garber committed the Austin House burglary."

"In whose interest, Edgar?"

"Well—apart from those who actually *did* commit the burglary—I am thinking of people who might want to discredit a firmly anti-Communist member of Congress."

"Who might that be?" asked the President, his patience wearing thin.

"The Communists, of course."

"Ah, yes," said the President. "A Red conspiracy. A rather convoluted one, though, don't you think? Let's see, in order to discredit Frank Garber, a group of conspirators commits a burglary in the south of England, smuggles a part of the loot into the United States, gives a large, well-known diamond to a hunt-club débutante in Vir-

inia, murders the congressman's son. . . . A little fantastic, isn't it,
dgar?"

"I have seen more fantastic things turn out to be true," said the
irector placidly.

"Of course," said the President, "*I* might have conspired with
hem myself, since Frank Garber has opposed important elements of
ay program."

Hoover smiled woodenly. "And of course," he said, "the conspira-
ors could be others. Germans . . . The congressman opposes Na-
ism, too."

"Philip Garber," said Mrs. Roosevelt firmly to the director, "*was* a
hief, Mr. Hoover. He paid his very considerable gambling debts by
elling the things he had stolen from other people. I am sorry for his
ather, but what I am telling you is a fact, supported by more than a
ew witnesses."

"I wish we could work together on this investigation, Mrs. Rooseelt," said Hoover.

"I've just given you an important piece of information," said she.
You can check it for yourself. Now, what can you give me?"

"Well . . . The Raphael diamond," said the director, "has been
xamined closely in our laboratory. There is something odd about it."

"Indeed?"

"Yes. The surface of the jewel bears faint traces of a peculiar sub-
tance. My lab technicians identified the substance as Ipana tooth-
aste. Why in the world do you suppose someone would put tooth-
aste on a big, valuable diamond?"

The President grinned. "To clean it, I should suppose."

The director of the F.B.I. nodded. "Yes, of course. But to clean off
hat?"

Mrs. Roosevelt clapped her hands. "Face cream, Mr. Hoover!" She
aughed. "Lavender-scented face cream!"

13

Mrs. Alicia Howell alternately frowned and grinned, her face entirely at the mercy of her emotions. Mrs. Roosevelt walked with her through the East Room.

"My God!" murmured Alicia Howell.

"Your husband served his country loyally for twenty-seven years, I believe it was," said Mrs. Roosevelt. "It is only appropriate that you should have a guided tour of the White House."

"I am grateful, Mrs. Roosevelt."

They walked through the Green Room and from there into the oval Blue Room. "President Cleveland was married in this room," said Mrs. Roosevelt. "He was the only President ever married in the White House."

"Oh," said Alicia Howell. "But where, then, was President Wilson married?"

"At Mrs. Galt's house," said Mrs. Roosevelt. "Not in the White House."

"Well, anyway," said Alicia Howell, looking around the Blue Room, "it's nicer to think about a wedding than about the funerals you said they had in the East Room. A funeral is sad and spooky, I don't care if it *was* Abraham Lincoln."

"Captain Howell is buried in Arlington, I suppose," said Mrs. Roosevelt.

"Yes . . . Yes."

Mrs. Roosevelt paused. "I have to ask you a difficult question," she said. "I am sorry, but I *must* ask it. What did you do with your dog? I mean, did you bury him somewhere, Mrs. Howell?"

"Cappy?" Alicia Howell whispered, frowning. "Why, I—I put him in the backyard, under that scrawny little tree back there. Why?"

"I must ask you to allow us to dig him up," said Mrs. Roosevelt. "I am terribly sorry to ask it, but it may mean all the difference for poor Pamela."

"Of course it would rain," grumbled Captain Kennelly. "If you had to do it with a human corpse, it would rain. In my life I've watched two exhumations, and both times it poured cats and—"

"Dogs," said Mrs. Roosevelt.

"Sorry," said Kennelly.

They stood under their big black umbrellas, beneath a purple-gray summer sky, and the rain fell in a steady, steaming torrent. Alicia Howell was not there. She had said she could not stand to see what they had to do, and she had gone to a movie. Sir Alan Burton stood nearer the two uniformed officers who were shoveling, critically watching as they turned over the earth under the little locust tree. He officiated over the exhumation of the dog Cappy just as he would have officiated, presumably, over the exhumation of a man or a woman. He had supervised the raking away of half a dozen tin cans and some scraps of sodden paper that had lain on the little grave, and by his stern expression he discouraged either complaints or jokes by the two policemen.

"She couldn't have buried it very deep," said Kennelly.

"She could have," said Mrs. Roosevelt. "A neighbor helped her."

Only one neighbor watched. Drake, the man Alicia Howell had at first accused of killing Cappy, stood in the doorway and scowled and shook his head. "I have long since ceased to be surprised at anything," he had said when they told him what they were doing.

Cappy, as they quickly learned, had not been buried deep. He had been buried in a cardboard box, which had deteriorated to a paper slurry mixed with soil in the weeks since the burial. Inside the box, fortunately, the dog had been wrapped in a fragment of quilted comforter. The comforter was intact, and the policemen were able to lift it out of the grave as a bundle.

Mrs. Roosevelt and Captain Kennelly stepped forward, almost involuntarily, as the policemen laid the rolled comforter on the ground and looked up at Sir Alan for further instructions.

"Unroll it," said the chief inspector from Scotland Yard.

The corpse of the black dog was infested with maggots but remained essentially whole. If it stank, the raindrops caught the rising stench and beat it to the ground. Cappy had been a medium-sized black mutt, as Alicia Howell had said. Sir Alan knelt beside it, careless of his umbrella, which he allowed to fall aside in the mud. From the voluminous pockets of his checked raincoat he took a large round magnifying glass and an oversized folding knife. Peering intently through the glass, he examined the dog's head.

"Ah," he said. "It would appear this was not a fool's errand after all."

"You've found it?" asked Mrs. Roosevelt.

"I believe I have," said Sir Alan.

He unfolded the knife, and with a long thin blade he pressed apart the stiff lips and the teeth of the dog. Once again he peered through the glass. He nodded.

"Have a look for yourself," he said, offering the glass to Mrs. Roosevelt. "Er . . . Captain Kennelly?"

The D.C. police captain knelt beside Sir Alan Burton. He, too, peered intently through the glass. He, too, nodded.

"Dark gray wool, then?" asked Mrs. Roosevelt.

"Yes," said Sir Alan. "It looks as though Mrs. Howell's doggy tore the pants of the man who killed him. Maybe more. A close examination of this animal's mouth may find traces of human blood."

"And if the wool is the same . . ."

Captain Kennelly nodded. "It would prove that the man who sat on Pamela Rush-Hodgeborne's sofa and left a bit of fabric from his pants also left a few threads in the mouth of this dog."

"It proves more than that," said Mrs. Roosevelt.

"It suggests more than that," said Kennelly.

"Well, *I* am satisfied," said Mrs. Roosevelt.

"Sir Burton?" said Kennelly. "What does it prove to you?"

"It proves to me that we have done a good afternoon's work here," said Sir Alan, "and that we deserve to get in out of the rain and have a spot of good hot English tea, with perhaps a taste of brandy."

The body of Cappy was removed to the naval laboratory where the bit of wool from Pamela's couch had been examined. The next day the laboratory reported that the wool entangled in the dog's teeth was identical. Also, the report said, traces of human blood were found in the dog's mouth.

Mrs. Roosevelt received the report just before she left the White House to be driven to the railroad station. She had received a call from New York the previous evening. The Countess of Crittenden had arrived on the *Ile de France* and was coming to Washington by train, arriving about noon.

This time it was not possible to evade reporters and photographers, and a score of them clustered around as the tall, formidable, blond countess stepped down from the train and embraced Mrs. Roosevelt on the platform.

"You here about the Pamela case?" one of the brasher reporters yelled.

The countess cast a calm, heavy-lidded gaze toward him. "I am here," she said, "quite unofficially. So unofficially, indeed, that *you* may regard me as not here at all."

So saying, the countess tossed her head to order her maid to follow, and she strode away with Mrs. Roosevelt—who, wisely for this occasion, had allowed herself to be shielded by two Secret Service agents.

"Does poor Pamela remain in prison?" the countess asked when she and Mrs. Roosevelt were settled in the back seat of the car.

"I am afraid she does, Rebecca. It all looks more and more hopeful for her, though."

"Will it be possible for me to visit her?"

"We will visit her this afternoon."

They saw her, as Mrs. Roosevelt usually did, through the bars of her cell. Pamela wept and reached through the bars to embrace the countess. The tall, silk-clad woman crushed the brim of her white straw hat against the steel bars to clasp Pamela to herself as best she could, and she patted her shoulder as though Pamela were her daughter and whispered softly to her. Mrs. Roosevelt stood aside, her eyes filled with tears.

When they returned to the White House, Mrs. Roosevelt telephoned Sir Alan Burton and asked him to come for tea. When, however, she told Rebecca, Countess of Crittenden, that she had a choice, perhaps, of taking tea or of joining the President for his early evening martinis, the countess expressed a firm preference for martinis. So it was that at six-thirty Sir Alan and the countess sat down with the President and Mrs. Roosevelt and Missy, and the countess watched fascinated as the President ritually mixed his favorite cocktail.

"That's a strong drink," Missy warned the countess as she accepted a martini from the President. "It's very American and may not be at all to your taste."

The countess sipped. "It is good," she said gravely.

Sir Alan Burton, too, accepted a martini. "After all," he remarked, "it is not often that one has the privilege of drinking a cocktail mixed by the President of the United States."

The conversation turned shortly to the murder of Philip Garber.

"I received a telephone call at my hotel in New York last evening," said the countess. "From Philip's father. He is most distressed that his son should be a suspect in the burglary. It is a wise child who knows his own father, they say, but in my experience it is a wise father who knows his son."

"What sort of fellow was Philip?" the President asked.

"A most engaging young man," said the countess. "Personable. Clever. A witty conversationalist. It was quite difficult at first for the earl and me to believe he let burglars into our house. We were all quite deceived by him—most of all, poor Pamela."

"I have brought with me," said Sir Alan, "a package of photographs, just arrived by aeroplane from London. They are photographs of people with criminal records, each of whom traveled from England to the States in the month prior to the murder of Philip Garber. Mrs. Roosevelt has seen the list. I should be grateful, Countess, if you would examine these photographs."

The pictures he handed her were not mug shots but oddly varied photographs, some clear, some fuzzy, taken of subjects in a variety of circumstances. There were a dozen or so of them, and the countess took a pince-nez from her handbag and squinted at each one in turn.

"Well, I have seen this man here," she said, handing Sir Alan one of the photographs.

"Indeed. In what circumstance, may I inquire?"

"He came to our house in London—twice, I believe—to see Philip. Polite, soft-spoken man, he was. He introduced himself as an Oxford don who had befriended Philip while he was studying there. You say the man has a criminal record? Lord, he *spoke* well enough to have been a don."

"His name is Harry Billingham," said Sir Alan. "He has a long arrest record. An unsavory character. Did you see Philip talk to him? Did they seem friendly?"

"Well, they—My God! This is Roland Pennington-Clarke! What sort of criminal record does Rolly have?"

Sir Alan took back the photograph and frowned over it. "Pennington-Clarke," he muttered. "Oh, yes. That is one of his names, I do recall. Roland Pennington-Clarke. He is known to Scotland Yard as Mayfair Jimmy more often than not. His actual name is James O'Neill. How is it that you know him, may I ask?"

"Why, he is assistant manager at one of the earl's clubs," said the countess. "The Ormsby Club, as a matter of fact. Do you know it, Sir Alan?"

"I do indeed, ma'am," said Sir Alan. "A gaming club, is it not?"

"Yes—and illegal, I suppose."

"Oh, yes. Quite."

"You say Rolly—or O'Neill—is in the States?" asked the countess.

"Yes. He was, anyway. A few weeks ago. Just before Philip Garber was murdered."

"Oh!" exclaimed the countess. "My God!"

"What is it, Rebecca?" asked Mrs. Roosevelt.

The countess shook her head. "What sort of criminal record does the man have?" she asked Sir Alan.

Sir Alan pursed his lips. "Well," he said, "Mayfair Jimmy is an all-'round hoodlum, you might say. He has served time in prison for robbery, forgery, assault. . . ."

"Then it is *he*, very likely, who murdered Philip Garber," said the countess.

"Why?"

The countess paused. She finished her first martini and, with a wan smile, handed the glass to the President. "The earl," she said, "came back from the club one evening with a strange story. It seems that this man—whatever his name—had asked him for a private meeting in an office at the club. The earl wondered if one of his checks had not been returned by the bank, but it was no such problem. No. It was something very different. Mr. Pennington-Clarke, as we know him, asked the earl if he was aware of how much money *his son* owed at the Ormsby Club. The earl laughed, of course, and said he had no son. At this, the man became angry and said a young man representing himself as our son had gambled at the tables in the club and lost almost a thousand pounds."

"Was it Philip?" asked the President.

"I'm afraid it was. He described the young man, and the earl immediately recognized the person described as Philip Garber. He told the man that not only was Philip Garber not our son but that Philip Garber was a chief suspect in the burglary at Austin House."

"Mayfair Jimmy was angry, you say?" asked Sir Alan.

"Very, according to the earl. He even had the temerity to suggest that the earl should pay the debt—though later he sought him out and apologized for having made such a suggestion."

"When had Philip incurred this debt, do you know?"

"Yes. It was just before he left for the States."

"After the burglary, then," said Mrs. Roosevelt.

"Yes," said the countess. She accepted a second martini from the President's shaker. "Mmm," she murmured as she sipped. "This is an American custom I could grow fond of. Even of the ice."

"It may be a coincidence, of course," said Sir Alan, "but it *is* suggestive, is it not, that Mayfair Jimmy O'Neill should travel to the States just after he learns that Philip Garber has swindled him out of a thousand pounds?"

"Tell me," said the President. "Did Mayfair Jimmy ever poison anyone?"

"Not that I know of, Mr. President."

"Well, I was thinking," said the President, tipping back his head and grinning, "how very neat a package of coincidences it would be if the man also had a record of committing murder by poison."

"I judge him capable of it," said Sir Alan grimly.

"Rolly? Capable of—Oh, dear," said the countess.

"And so is Harry Billingham," said Sir Alan.

"And so is Gully Balzac," said Mrs. Roosevelt.

Sir Alan shrugged. "Then let us not overlook Cynthia Dawes."

"And there remains, unhappily," said the President, "one more suspect we must not overlook. Pretty little Pamela. Philip did die in her apartment, after drinking what she served him."

"Oh but, Franklin," protested Mrs. Roosevelt. "There are so many others who had *motive* for killing him."

"I am not at all sure you've exhausted the list," said the President. "There may be others. Indeed, it would appear that everyone who ever knew Philip Garber sooner or later had reason to want him dead."

"The problem," said the countess, "is to prove that someone other than poor Pamela actually *did it.*"

"You may never have to prove that," said the President. "The list of suspects is becoming so long and crowded that Pamela may simply be lost in the crowd."

"But *Pamela,*" said Mrs. Roosevelt indignantly, "remains in *jail,* while the others are at liberty. That is an injustice I, for one, will not continue to tolerate."

The President lifted his glass. "To you, then," he said. "To your success."

14

Betty McDougal, otherwise known as Désirée LaFlamme, put her cigarette in her mouth with two fingers of her right hand. She was handcuffed, and she frowned for a moment over the faint red mark of the cuff on her right wrist. She slipped that cuff up her arm and then slid the other one up and down, looking for a similar mark and not finding one.

They were sitting in a room in the Mayflower Hotel—Mrs. Roosevelt, Sir Alan Burton, Captain Edward Kennelly, and J. Edgar Hoover, as well as Betty McDougal. It was a meeting on what Hoover had called—somewhat melodramatically, Mrs. Roosevelt thought—"neutral ground."

"You don't want to go back for a long sentence, do you, Betty?" said Kennelly.

Betty McDougal rubbed her eyes with her knuckles. She had been crying a few minutes before, and her eyes were still wet. "No," she whispered weakly.

"Like half your life," said Kennelly.

She shook her head. "No!"

Captain Kennelly turned down the corners of his mouth and shrugged at the others.

"Let's bring in the stenographer," said Director Hoover.

Hoover, in a light blue suit, white shirt, and bright red satin necktie, had scowled through the meeting so far. Mrs. Roosevelt had kept a skeptical frown on her face, even though what they had heard so far was good news for Pamela Rush-Hodgeborne. She had a small notepad poised on her knee and was scribbling notes in the manner of a newspaper reporter. Only Sir Alan Burton was unmoved by the meeting and sat as if he were a faintly bemused witness to proceedings that meant little to him.

Kennelly opened the door and admitted a tall young woman with red hair, the stenographer. He helped her arrange a chair near a table and waited while she took two notepads from her large straw bag and spread half a dozen pencils within easy reach on the table. When she was ready, she smiled faintly and nodded at Kennelly.

"Okay," said Kennelly brusquely. "Put down the date and time. Make the place my office, D.C. police headquarters. Pick it up from there. Betty, tell us your name."

Betty McDougal shrugged. "Betty McDougal," she said.

"You make this statement, your own free will, right?"

"I guess."

"Yes or no."

"Yes."

"Okay. Who killed Philip Garber?"

"Gully Balzac," said Betty McDougal.

The stenographer raised a hand. "Uh?"

"G-U-L-L-Y B-A-L-Z-A-C," said Kennelly. "He do it all by himself?"

"No, he hired a guy to do it."

"Who?"

"I don't know the guy's name."

"Why'd he kill him?"

"Long story," said Betty McDougal.

With the exception of the stenographer, who was hardly able to conceal her amazement at this dialogue, no one was surprised. They had come to this hotel room for a secret meeting with Betty McDougal—and with Cynthia Dawes, who was waiting in the adjacent room —because yesterday she had told Captain Kennelly privately that Gully Balzac had killed Philip Garber and that she wanted to negotiate a deal for a light sentence in return for her sworn statement. She had insisted she would make her formal statement only in the presence of Mrs. Roosevelt and J. Edgar Hoover.

She sniffed and wiped her mouth with the back of her hand. She was wearing a red-and-white flowered dress and white shoes. She had insisted, Kennelly had reported before she was brought to the room, that she be allowed to put on makeup before she left the jail, and her mouth was heavily colored with bright red lipstick.

"Where do you want to start, Betty?" asked Kennelly.

She shrugged.

"Tell us about the Raphael—R-A-P-H-A-E-L—diamond, then," said Kennelly.

Betty McDougal drew a deep breath. "Phil brought it in," she said. "He owed Gully a bundle, and he tried to pay him off with the diamond, said it was worth maybe fifteen, twenty grand. Gully had taken merchandise from him before, but Gully took one look at that rock and told Phil not even to bring it in the club. Later on, Phil showed the diamond to me and asked me what I could get him for it. I'd bought merchandise from him before. I told him I'd ask around, but he said he didn't have much time, he had to have the money fast. I made a couple calls, but the word was out that Phil Garber was trouble, and nobody wanted anything from him."

"What kind of trouble?" asked Hoover.

"The word was around that he'd pulled off a big job in England and brought back a load of hot jewels but that some of them were too hot to handle."

"Are you saying," asked the director, "that Philip Garber was a known jewel thief?"

She nodded. "Definitely."

"Go on."

She ground out her cigarette in an ashtray. "Can you let me have another smoke?" she asked.

Kennelly tapped a Camel out of a pack and handed it to her. She held her chained hands to her mouth and accepted a light from his lighter.

"Nobody was willing to fence the Raphael diamond, then?" asked Sir Alan.

Betty McDougal shook her head. "They didn't know the diamond by name, but they knew a big diamond from Phil would have to be red hot."

"So why did you take it?" asked Kennelly.

"I had a buyer for it," said Betty McDougal.

"Cynthia Dawes," said Kennelly. "D-A-W-E-S."

"Right," said Betty McDougal. "I knew she wouldn't put it back on

he market. She wanted it for herself. I never thought she'd try to
lave the thing *set.*"

"How did you know she wanted it?" asked Mrs. Roosevelt.

"Phil told me how he'd got it back from her—and how mad she was
o have to give it up. I knew her. She'd been in the club. She liked to
ee me strip. It gave her some kind of thrill. She liked to feel how
much better than me she was."

"So what did you pay him for it?"

"A couple thousand. I borrowed a thousand from Gully. I had a
housand of my own."

"Gully knew you were buying the diamond?"

"He knew. He didn't like the deal much. He said it amounted to
Phil paying Gully with Gully's own money. But he went along anyway."

"Okay, so you bought the diamond from Garber for two thousand.
How much did Cynthia pay you for it?"

"Four thousand."

"You repaid Gully?"

"I paid him twelve hundred—the grand plus interest."

"And Philip Garber paid Gully Balzac two thousand?"

"No. That was what made Gully mad. That was the last straw, as
you might say. When Phil got the two grand from me, he didn't give
it to Gully. He owed Gully eleven thousand five hundred—something like that—and he didn't even give Gully the two he got for the
diamond. That really blew Gully's cork."

"So what makes you think Gully had Garber killed?" asked Kennelly.

"He threatened to. He told Phil that he'd have every bone in Phil's
body broke. He said he'd show him what it was to welsh on Gully
Balzac. Then, after Phil was dead—I mean, after it came out in the
papers that Phil was dead—he told me, 'See what happens to guys
that play funny games with Gully Balzac.'"

"All of this," said Sir Alan, "falls short of proving that Balzac had
Philip Garber murdered. Tell me, Miss McDougal, if you will please,
what other, more direct evidence you have to offer."

Betty McDougal put her cigarette to her lips and took a deep drag.
"The guy came to the club," she said. "The guy Gully hired to do it, I
mean."

"How do you know this guy was hired by Gully to murder Garber?" asked Kennelly.

"I had to entertain the guy," she said. "You know what I mean? I was doin' my strip—like you saw me do that night when you came to the club—and Gully called me over and told me to sit down with him and this guy. They were drinkin'. I had to drink with them. I thought I recognized him, and after I heard them talk awhile, I knew for sure who he was. He was a mob guy from Baltimore. Phil wouldn't be the first guy he killed."

"Did you hear them actually discuss murdering Philip Garber?" asked Sir Alan.

"Sure," said Betty McDougal positively. "They talked about knockin' Phil off because Phil was a welsher."

"Describe the man," said Sir Alan.

"Weaselly-looking guy," she said. "You know. Short. Little. Nasty little face."

"But you don't know his name," said Kennelly.

She shook her head.

"How did he kill Philip Garber, Betty?" asked Director Hoover.

"He poisoned him," she said.

"Odd way for a mob enforcer to kill a man," said Hoover.

She shrugged.

Hoover stood. He looked down at Betty, his face coldly scornful. "You've done time in two penitentiaries," he said. "Haven't you?"

She nodded.

"You have a record of other arrests. Petty theft . . ."

She nodded again.

"You're a small-time crook, aren't you?"

Betty McDougal sighed. "If you say so," she muttered.

"Now the Raphael diamond has been traced to you, and you face a long term. Don't you?"

The young woman's face softened and turned red, and she sniffed and once more nodded.

"So you want a deal," said Hoover.

She looked up into his face. Her eyes were wet with new tears. "Yeah," she whispered.

"So you'll tell any lie you think will please," said Hoover, and abruptly he sat down again and turned his face away from Betty

McDougal. "I don't think I really care what she says," he told the others.

"Off the record," said Kennelly to the stenographer. "You'll testify to what you've told us, won't you, Betty?"

She nodded and whispered, "You . . . said . . ."

"I said we'd let you cop a plea for receiving," said Kennelly. "We'll drop whatever else we've got on you. One to three, I suppose. You'll get one to three."

Betty McDougal sobbed. "My record, I'll have to do the three," she wailed.

"Your record, you could go up for life under the Habitual Criminals Act," said Hoover sullenly. "I think somebody's doing you a big favor."

Betty McDougal covered her mouth with one hand, her cigarette protruding between two fingers; with the other she covered her eyes. She wept.

Captain Kennelly stepped to the door and spoke into the adjacent room. A matron entered to take Betty McDougal in custody and lead her away. Another matron led in Cynthia Dawes. The two young women brushed past each other in the doorway, each jerking angrily and scornfully away from the other.

Cynthia Dawes gaped when she saw who faced her. Her wide eyes passed from Captain Kennelly to Mrs. Roosevelt, then to Director Hoover, then to Sir Alan Burton, then back to Mrs. Roosevelt. Her face glowed red.

"Sit down, Cynthia," said Captain Kennelly.

Cynthia was wearing a cream-white linen dress, open-toed high-heel shoes, and sheer silk stockings. She wore no makeup, and her face looked pale. She, too, was handcuffed, and her fists were clenched angrily at her waist. She sat down reluctantly, rigidly erect. She glanced around, resentful but at the same time so deeply embarrassed to be sitting there in a prisoner's manacles that Mrs. Roosevelt was moved to sympathy.

"You said you'd give us a statement," said Captain Kennelly. "The stenographer is ready."

" 'Fore I do," said Cynthia, "I want t' be sure everythin's understood."

"All right," said Kennelly. "The Virginia authorities have agreed.

You're going to give us a full statement about how you came to have the Raphael diamond. Then you're going to tell us all you know about the murder of Philip Garber. You're going to plead guilty to receiving stolen property. The district attorney over in Fairfax County is going to recommend to the judge that you be placed on probation. I'll recommend it. Director Hoover will recommend it."

"Miz Roosevelt . . . ?" asked Cynthia.

"No," said Kennelly firmly. "Her name is not to be used in any way."

Cynthia Dawes exhaled sharply. "What choice have I got?" she asked.

"You can go to trial if you're innocent," said Kennelly blandly. "That's what you should do if you're innocent."

Cynthia Dawes shot him a baleful glance. "If I was *innocent* of receivin' a stolen diamond," she said, "you all can be sure my daddy would be *suin'* every one of you."

"But you're not," said Kennelly. "Let's get your statement down. Tell the stenographer your name."

"Cynthia Dawes."

"When and how did you first see the Raphael diamond?"

She recited the story they had heard before, of how Philip Garber had given her the diamond for an engagement ring, then had demanded she return it so he could pay a gambling debt, and how then she had bought it from Betty McDougal, to whom Garber had sold it.

"Where did Philip Garber get the diamond, Cynthia?" asked Kennelly.

"I sincerely don't know."

"Cynthia . . ."

"Well. When he gave it t' me for an engagement ring, he never told me he'd stolen it. I would never have accepted a stolen diamond for my engagement ring. But when he wanted it back, he told me. He said he was poor. He said his daddy wouldn't give him much. He said he'd stolen things once in a while to get enough money to live well. He said the diamond had belonged to a rich old man in England that kept it hidden in a safe all the time, so nobody ever saw it. He said he'd had a chance to take it, and he took it. He said he wanted sombody to have it that would know how to appreciate it. He was lyin' when he said that."

"So then you knew it was stolen property," said Kennelly.

Cynthia nodded. "I knew it from then on," she said.

"So when you bought it from Betty McDougal, you knew you were buying a stolen diamond."

"Yes. An' that's the crime I committed, I guess. That's why I'm in jail," said Cynthia sadly.

"You knew it was worth much more than you paid for it."

She nodded. "We're not poor, my family," she said. "But I could never have owned a diamond like that except . . ."

"Except by trading in stolen goods," said Kennelly.

"Yes," she agreed quietly. "It's a *beautiful* thing, though, isn't it? Beautiful—"

Director Hoover interrupted. "Do you know, of your own personal knowledge, that Philip Garber stole other jewelry or had other stolen jewelry in his possession?"

Cynthia frowned. Her eyes narrowed. "Is this gonna get me in *more* trouble?" she asked.

Hoover shook his head. "Not unless you helped him steal it or fence it."

The young woman frowned. "He had different jewelry, different times. He tried to use it to pay gamblin' debts. I didn't know it was stolen at the time. I guess I figured it out, though, by 'n' by."

Hoover's grim face darkened all the more.

Kennelly nodded. "All right. Now. You know Gully Balzac, don't you?"

She nodded. "Yes. Sure. I been in his place lots of times."

"Did Gully Balzac kill Philip Garber?"

"I wouldn't know. I don't know who killed him."

"Gully threatened him, though, didn't he? In your hearing?"

"I reckon you could call it that. But Phil didn't take it very serious. He wasn't afraid of him at all."

"Tell us about it," said Kennelly. "Tell us about Gully's threats and how Phil reacted."

"Phil owed all around, y' know," she said. "He didn't have any sense at all 'bout gamblin'. I was with him one night when he won six thousand dollars. You'd thought he'd died and gone t' heaven. Couldn't stop talkin' 'bout it. Never *did* stop talkin' 'bout it. But, y' know, he'd *lost* many times that, over the years. He *owed* more'n that. But that's all he thought of—how he'd won one time. He . . ."

As she warmed to the subject of Garber's gambling, Cynthia tried to emphasize her words with gestures of her hands, but the handcuffs frustrated her. Her gestures were pulled up short by hard jerks. She stopped speaking, stared at the handcuffs, and her face turned hot red. "Oh, why can't you take these horrible things *off* me?" she cried.

"Why not, indeed, Captain?" asked Mrs. Roosevelt.

Kennelly nodded. "Okay," he said. He pulled a ring of keys from his jacket pocket, and with one of them he unlocked the handcuffs and put them aside on the table.

Rubbing her wrists, regaining a measure of calm, Cynthia spoke quietly. "One night," she said, "I was with Phil at Gully's place, and Gully came to the blackjack table where Phil and I were playin' and asked us to come with him. We went over to his table, and he took Phil's markers out of his pocket and laid them out on the table. They came to almost ten thousand dollars. Gully looked at me and said, 'You always pay up, Cynthia. Maybe you ought to pay up for Phil, 'cause if you don't or somebody don't, he's in trouble.' "

"Meaning what?" asked Kennelly.

She smiled cynically. "You weren't born yesterday, Captain. You know what it means."

"What did Phil say?" asked Hoover.

"You aren't gonna like what he said," she replied, looking at Hoover. "He reminded Gully his daddy was a member of the Congress, and he said it wouldn't be smart for anybody to do anythin' to him."

"And what did Gully say to that?" asked Hoover.

"Said that didn't make any difference. Then Phil said his daddy's *friends* wouldn't like it if Gully got tough, said his daddy had friends that knew how to break bones, too. But Gully said there wasn't anybody would stick up for a welsher."

The director rose again, this time only to take a stand at the window and look down at the street.

"You know what he thought?" Cynthia asked, turning in her chair to speak to Hoover. "He thought he was gonna *win* enough, sooner or later, to pay off every cent he owed. That's how he figured he was gonna pay it."

Sir Alan Burton spoke. "Did Gully Balzac ever say in your hearing,

Miss Dawes—specifically and in so many words—that he would do physical harm to Philip Garber or would arrange to have it done to him?"

Cynthia nodded. "Well . . . yes. I don't know how serious it was. It wasn't that same night that I was talkin' about before. It was later. He told Phil he'd see to it that every bone in his body was broke if Phil didn't pay up and pay up soon."

"And what did Philip Garber say to that?"

"He just laughed at Gully and told him it wasn't a good idea to get tough with Phil Garber."

"When was this?"

"Week or ten days before Phil was murdered."

"Were you in love with Philip, Cynthia?" asked Mrs. Roosevelt gently.

"Once . . . yes," she said quietly. "Then I found out about him. How could a girl stay in love with a man like he was?"

"May I assume now," said Mrs. Roosevelt after Cynthia Dawes was once again handcuffed and was taken from the room, "that charges against Pamela will now be dropped?"

"No," said Captain Kennelly. "I can't do that. But I'll go along with her being released on bail. What's more, we'll have her trial postponed." With his hands clasped before his chin, he shook his head. "I can't charge Gully Balzac, either."

"Betty McDougal is going to spend the next five days looking at mug shots," said Hoover. "She's going to look at every mob-connected face in the file. If she can't come up with her weaselly-looking little man with the nasty face, I'll know she's lying."

"If in fact you come up with an identification, Director," said Sir Alan, "let's let Pamela's neighbors have a look at the photos."

"Well, tell me something, Sir Alan," said Hoover. "Do you think Betty will make an identification?"

"I'm afraid I don't," said Sir Alan.

15

The President had finished with his breakfast tray, and it was now at the foot of the bed. He sat almost erect in the middle of a clutter of newspapers, with pillows plumped behind his back to hold him up. The First Lady, fully dressed and in a white straw hat, stood near the foot of the bed, having a few words with him before she went out.

"The odd thing," she said, pulling on her white gloves, "is that this man Balzac so immediately fled. They don't have any evidence against him. Still, he seems to have disappeared."

"Guilty conscience," suggested the President.

"Don't they simply have to drop the charges against Pamela now?"

"Well," said the President, "it's a little hard to overlook the fact that Philip Garber died in her apartment of poison found in a drink she mixed him. Whose fault would it be if someone died from one of my martinis?"

"It would be the fault of someone who meddled with the ingredients," said Mrs. Roosevelt emphatically.

The President nodded. "That's a compelling point, Babs," he said. "*I* think so."

"Well, anyway, Pamela's being released on bail tomorrow?"

"As soon as Rebecca's London bank transfers the funds. The Dawes girl is out already," said Mrs. Roosevelt. "There's irony there, don't you think?"

"Irony? Oh, yes. The whole case is filled with irony."

"Funny . . ." mused Mrs. Roosevelt.

The President smiled broadly. "You want to hear something funny, Babs?" he asked. "The head of the British delegation to Moscow—the one that's going to try to head off some kind of *rapprochement* between Hitler and Stalin—is a very able man, I'm sure, but his name is Admiral Sir Reginald Aylmer Ranfurly Plunkett-Ernle-Erle-Drax. Voroshilov will fall asleep during the introduction, and the admiral will be so tired from carrying his name to Moscow he'll need two days' rest before they can get the conference started."

Mrs. Roosevelt glanced at her wristwatch. *"Rapprochement,"* she said, frowning. "Between Hitler and Stalin. . . . Do you think there's any serious likelihood?"

"Yes," said the President. "I'm afraid there is."

"It will mean war," she said grimly. "And here I am, asking you to give your attention to the personal tragedy of one English girl."

"When you and I, Babs, can't find time to do what we can to help a friendless girl who needs us, then we'll be a poor sort of people to be leading a nation," said the President. "Keep at it, old girl, and keep me informed of what happens."

Mrs. Roosevelt, Rebecca, Countess of Crittenden, and Sir Alan Burton sat in Pamela's living room, in her apartment, the next afternoon. Pamela was in the bathtub, not luxuriating—as she insisted—but trying to wash the stench of the jail off her skin and out of her hair. They had been waiting for her here at noon, when Captain Kennelly delivered her home, having succeeded in slipping her out of the jail and into his car without any reporters getting wind of it. He had stayed to talk only for a few minutes, saying he had obligations to meet.

"I am deeply concerned," said Mrs. Roosevelt, "that Pamela should not sleep alone in this apartment."

"I agree totally," said the countess, though it was not clear from her tone and expression whether she shared Mrs. Roosevelt's concern or was commenting on the quality of the living quarters.

"Since we continue in the dark, really, as to who murdered Philip Garber, we cannot be certain that whoever it was did not mean to murder Pamela too—or that he may not return and try again."

"It is true," said Sir Alan. "We cannot be certain."

"Then it would be dangerous for her to stay here."

"Yes," said Sir Alan.

Mrs. Roosevelt frowned. "It will be difficult," she said thoughtfully, "for me to have her as an employee or as a guest at the White House, in view of the fact that she is only free on bail and remains a suspect in a first-degree homicide."

"I was offered accommodation with our dear friend Andrea Bianchi," said the countess. "I declined only because I had your kind invitation to stay at the White House. I am certain Andrea would be pleased to have Pamela as her guest for a while, particularly if—as we must insist—her whereabouts remain secret until the whole unpleasantness about Philip Garber is one way or the other resolved."

"I have a very different idea, if I may say so," said Sir Alan. "With all respect, ladies, I think it important that Miss Rush-Hodgeborne maintain *the appearance* of living here. What a very positive development it would be if our villain were to come here some night to attempt to kill Miss Rush-Hodgeborne and instead deliver himself into our hands."

"You mean to use Pamela as a decoy?" asked the countess.

Sir Alan nodded. "Except that she will not be here," he said.

"Then how is the appearance to be maintained?" asked Mrs. Roosevelt.

"We must find another flat here where she may spend her nights," said Sir Alan. "If the building is watched, it will be noticed that she is still inside. Our villain, however, will not know what flat she occupies. He will come to this one, where he will be confronted not by the charming Miss Rush-Hodgeborne but by a burly policeman."

"Alicia Howell," said Mrs. Roosevelt. "She should stay upstairs with Mrs. Howell."

When Pamela came out of the bathroom, Alicia Howell was with the others in the living room.

"Oh, I am *so* sorry about Cappy," said Pamela as she embraced Alicia Howell. "I can't help but feel some responsibility."

"Poor little Cappy," said Alicia Howell. "Anyway, he bit whoever it was killed Phil."

"Would that *I* could bite him," said Pamela.

"It was hard for me to sleep nights, thinking of you in jail," said Alicia Howell.

"It was difficult for *me* to sleep nights being there, you may believe," Pamela said, sighing.

Pamela, wearing a red skirt and a white blouse, ran a comb through her wet hair as they talked. She had gained weight during her weeks of enforced inactivity, and she had a fleshy look. Mrs. Roosevelt, studying her now, here in her apartment, saw in her a certain furtive, sly look she had never noticed before, and for a brief moment she wondered if she had not placed too much faith in Pamela's innocence. She remained firm in her judgment that Pamela had not murdered Philip, but she found herself wondering if Pamela had not, just possibly, taken some role in the Austin House burglary. Pamela had shown this afternoon a defiant independence of spirit that Mrs. Roosevelt had not expected. She seemed to believe she had gained a special wisdom from her weeks in jail, and she expressed what Mrs. Roosevelt considered an unfortunate confidence in the opinions given her by the women who had spoken to her from nearby cells.

"I can't go home," Pamela said. "It was explained to me that I must remain in the States, actually here in Washington. I am not sure how they expect me to live. A person who has spent time in jail has very limited horizons so far as employment is concerned."

"You are still employed by me, dear," said Mrs. Roosevelt. "Your wages have continued even while you were in jail, so you have some money coming."

"How very kind!" said Pamela, surprised and sincere. "Still, what work can I do now? You *can't* want me at the White House. After all, I am a suspect in a heinous crime."

"We shall find work for you," said Mrs. Roosevelt. "You will earn your wages. And now Sir Alan wants to talk with you about a scheme of his for solving the mystery of Philip's death."

Tommy Thompson led J. Edgar Hoover into Mrs. Roosevelt's office. Hoover shook Mrs. Roosevelt's hand and seated himself in the chair she indicated, facing her where she sat at her breakfront desk.

"I am afraid," he said without preliminaries, "I must give up the idea of saving the reputation of Philip Garber. I hope you can understand how I regarded it as a duty to protect, as much as I could, the name of a prominent member of Congress."

"I *quite* understand, Mr. Hoover," said she with a broad, warm smile.

"You are an understanding lady," he said.

"I have made my own errors, Mr. Hoover," she said. "It would ill behoove me to focus too much attention on those of others."

The director's nod amounted to a shallow bow. "I have some information that may be of interest to you," he said.

"Ah," said she. "I am afraid I have nothing new to convey to you."

"Nonetheless," said Hoover, again nodding gravely. "Betty McDougal is very positive in her identification of the man she says she heard discussing the death of Philip Garber with Gully Balzac. We haven't been able to shake her story. With the disappearance of Balzac, it is not as easy as it was before to discount what she says."

"I remain unwilling to believe her," said Mrs. Roosevelt. "As much as I would like to."

Hoover lifted his eyebrows. "The man she identifies is a certain Frederick Moellenkopf, known as Freddy the Melon. He's a mob enforcer from Baltimore, like she says. She picked out his picture without knowing who the picture was of. Balzac is a small-time operator for the Baltimore mob. It's not unlikely they would send Freddy the Melon to collect debts for him."

"Do you suppose this Freddy wears Scottish woolens?" asked Mrs. Roosevelt.

The director smiled faintly. "Sir Alan told me about the dog and the torn pants. I'm having Baltimore tailor shops checked for repairs to dark gray Scottish-wool suits."

"Well," said Mrs. Roosevelt with a slight shrug, "at any rate, Pamela is out of jail, as is Cynthia Dawes. That leaves only poor Betty McDougal."

"Right now you couldn't *shove* Betty McDougal out the door of the D.C. jail," said Hoover.

"Oh?"

"She'd be scared to death to go on the street."

"Oh, because—"

"Because she fingered Gully Balzac and Freddy the Melon."

Mrs. Roosevelt frowned and nodded. "The name Gully, incidentally," she said. "For Gulliver?"

Hoover grinned. "For Guglielmo," he said.

"Oh, Mrs. Roosevelt," said Pamela late that afternoon. "If not for you, I should most certainly have been convicted of murder and sent o my death in the electric chair. As 'tis, not only do I have your fine nd sympathetic help, and the help of the countess, but my case is eing investigated by the director of the F.B.I. and a chief inspector f Scotland Yard. I dread to think what should have happened—"

"It was a duty," interrupted Mrs. Roosevelt. "Doing justice is always a duty."

They sat in Pamela's apartment, with a pot of tea and cups on the mall table before the couch. Pamela poured and handed a cup to Mrs. Roosevelt.

"Wait!" said Pamela suddenly. "I . . . ." She licked her lips. "I shall ample the tea from each cup."

Mrs. Roosevelt sipped tea. "I have perfect confidence in you, 'amela," she said.

Pamela's eyes widened. "I have washed every dish," she said. Thoroughly."

"Of course."

"The sugar," said Pamela. "And the milk. I bought them today."

"I'm sure you did," said Mrs. Roosevelt, with a smile. "The police eft nothing in your pantry."

"Well, I'm glad of that. I wouldn't have dared to use anything."

Mrs. Roosevelt was experiencing one more small surprise about 'amela Rush-Hodgeborne. The girl was wearing blue shorts that left er legs bare below mid-thigh. Buttons on the shorts were placed in he manner of the buttons on a sailor's bell-bottom trousers, and her louse was white, with a big flat sailor collar hanging down the back. he outfit seemed more than a little immodest to Mrs. Roosevelt, articularly in view of the fact that they expected a number of visiors to the flat. But she attributed her surprise—and Pamela's choice f an outfit—to the difference in their ages, and determined not to espect the bare-legged girl less. Though in some ways Pamela eemed the very image of a proper English girl, she *had*, Mrs. Rooseelt recalled, admitted Philip Garber to her bedroom and bed, even fter she knew she would never marry him. It was difficult sometimes o be tolerant of the conduct of this generation, even more than of he generation of the so-called Roaring Twenties, but Mrs. Roosevelt vas sternly determined to live in each decade as it came, without ondemning.

Sir Alan Burton arrived a little after five-thirty. "The director and

the captain have asked me to attend this meeting without them," h
said. His face was flushed, and his breath was fragrant with the odo
of Scotch whisky. "It seems they have a degree of confidence in th
professional competence of the Yard. Tea? Thank you. Have you a to
of whisky by any chance? I mean, *whisky*, not any of that god-awfu
American stuff—forgive me, Mrs. Roosevelt." He sat down, plump
and ruddy. "Just a tot, Pamela. No more."

"I'm afraid I haven't anything, Sir Alan," said Pamela. "It was al
taken, you know."

"Ah, to be sure," he said. "To see if any further bottles contained
whiff of potassium cyanide. I'd drink that in preference to *bourbon*
let me tell you. Ah, well . . . tea."

As he was sipping his tea, there was a timid rap on the door, an
Pamela opened it to admit Alicia Howell.

"We should be very grateful," said Sir Alan after Alicia Howell wa
seated and had a cup of tea in her hands, "if you would glance ove
some photographs we have. Never mind for the moment who th
people in the pictures might be. Just tell us, Mrs. Howell, if you will, i
you have ever seen any of them before."

Alicia Howell frowned over each of a dozen photographs. As sh
put each aside, Sir Alan handed it to Mrs. Roosevelt, so she coul
know who the subjects were. Mrs. Roosevelt recognized some of th
faces. There was Harry Billingham, the London hoodlum who hac
presented himself at Crittenden House as an Oxford don. There wa
James O'Neill, alias Mayfair Jimmy, alias Roland Pennington-Clarke
the assistant manager of the Ormsby Club. There was Cynthi
Dawes, and Betty McDougal. There was Guglielmo "Gully" Balzac
There was a man with a cruel, pinched face, whom she took to b
Frederick Moellenkopf, alias Freddy the Melon. The rest were un
known to her.

"Well, I know one of them," said Alicia Howell after she had looke
through the whole dozen.

"Which?" asked Sir Alan.

Alicia Howell reached across the table and picked up the picture o
Cynthia Dawes. "This one," she said.

"Ah, yes," said Sir Alan. "Philip brought her here one evening. Sh
spent the night with him in this flat."

"I wouldn't know about that," said Alicia Howell. "I saw her on th street once and in the hall once, both times in the afternoon, not at night."

"Are you certain?" asked Sir Alan.

"Absolutely," said Alicia Howell. "Well dressed. Uppity. I remember her all right."

Sir Alan grimaced and shook his head. "Somehow I wish you didn't," he said. He glanced from Pamela to Mrs. Roosevelt. "Oh, dear," he murmured. "Cynthia, too. Oh, my."

Their next visitor rapped firmly on the door. When Alicia Howell saw who it was, she rose, smiled wanly at Pamela, and left as the man entered.

"Good evening, Mrs. Howell," the man said.

"Good evening, Mr. Drake," she said coldly.

Drake turned and watched Alicia Howell retreat with rapid steps along the hall. He shrugged. "Strange woman," he said.

"Good evening, sir," said Sir Alan. "Mr. Alfred Drake, I believe?"

The sixty-year-old man nodded vaguely at Sir Alan and turned his attention quickly to Pamela, conspicuously eyeing her shorts and her pale legs. He was—as Pamela had explained earlier—a man who was shaved only by a barber and only twice a week, and this evening seemed to be two or three days after his last shave. White stubble stood on his cheeks and chin. He was dressed in a dark blue double-breasted suit, nonetheless, and his necktie was tightly knotted.

"A cup of tea, Mr. Drake?" Pamela asked.

Drake opened his mouth to answer just as his eyes stopped on Mrs. Roosevelt. *"My God, Eleanor Roosevelt!"* he exclaimed.

Mrs. Roosevelt smiled and laughed. "Mr. Drake," she said. "How very nice of you to come."

"How nice of *you*," said Drake. "Pamela told me . . . but I didn't believe it. It's an honor, ma'am."

"Please sit down, Mr. Drake," said Mrs. Roosevelt. "We've looked forward to meeting you. I don't believe we have introduced Sir Alan Burton, chief inspector of Scotland Yard."

"Scotland Yard!" said Drake happily. "I've read every *word* that's ever been printed about Sherlock Holmes. Sir Alan . . . ?"

"Burton," said Sir Alan dryly.

"Er . . . tea, Mr. Drake?" asked Pamela.

"Tea," said Drake, with a small frown. "You don't happen to have a nip of something stronger, do you?"

"I'm afraid not."

"If you're thinking of whisky," said Sir Alan, "so am I. Unfortunately, she hasn't a drop in the house."

"I'll remedy that," said Drake firmly. "In a minute. Up to my place and back, in just a minute."

Drake hurried out, and in the minute he was gone Sir Alan sipped sparingly of his tea and smiled benignly.

"He's the man Mrs. Howell at first supposed might have killed her dog, you remember," Mrs. Roosevelt reminded Sir Alan.

"But he didn't," said Sir Alan.

"Well," said Mrs. Roosevelt, "I should be curious to know if he has a dark gray Scottish-wool suit."

Drake bustled back in, carrying a bottle by the neck. "Old Granddad," he said, with a proud smile. "The head of the bourbon family."

Mrs. Roosevelt laughed, but Drake did not notice as he poured generous splashes of bourbon into the two glasses Pamela provided. He lifted his glass in toast and watched Sir Alan drink from his.

"The very best," said Drake. "Nothin' but."

Putting a good face on it, Sir Alan smiled weakly and swallowed the whiskey. "You understand, of course, what we're here to discuss," he said.

"The murder," said Drake.

"The murder," said Sir Alan.

"I heard nothin'," said Drake. "Saw nothin'. I told the police. I'm sorry, Pamela. I wish I had. Nothin' would suit me better than to be able to say I saw someone else come in here and kill Garber."

"The night when Mrs. Howell's dog was killed," said Sir Alan, "Did you hear him bark?"

"Of course I heard him bark," said Drake. He tipped the bottle over his and Sir Alan's empty glasses. "There was never an hour of my life, for six years, I didn't hear that dog bark. But I heard nothin' special that night. She accused me of breaking her dog's neck, you know. I was tempted, I'll admit, but I didn't kill it. If I'd been going to do that, I'd have done it years ago."

"I'd like to ask you, Mr. Drake, to look over some photographs," said Sir Alan. "Just tell me if you've ever seen any of these people before."

"Sure. Drink up while I look," said Drake.

He reached into the pocket of his jacket and extracted a pair of steel-rimmed round spectacles, and with them in place on his nose, he peered intently at the pictures, one by one.

"Well, I've seen this fellow," he said after a minute.

Sir Alan picked up the photograph that Drake had tossed across the table. "Where?" Sir Alan asked. "And when?"

Drake reached for the picture and looked at it again. "On the street outside," he said. "Two or three times. I remember him very well. Each time he was carryin' a bag of groceries, but each time he was staring around like he didn't know where he was. I thought that was very odd, wouldn't you?"

"Why?" asked Sir Alan.

"Well," said Drake, "if you were carryin' home a bag of groceries, wouldn't you know where you were? Wouldn't you know where you lived? If you were carryin' it to somebody else's place, like a member of your family, or a friend, you might be lost on the street once, but the second time you'd know where you were, wouldn't you? Wouldn't you?"

"Can you remember how the man was dressed?" asked Sir Alan.

Drake shrugged. "Ordinary. Suit, I guess. Hat. Oh, yes, I remember the hat. Black. Style you call—homburg, I think. Don't see many of those on the street."

"The suit," said Sir Alan. "Do you recall anything about the suit?"

Drake shook his dead. "Nothing special," he said. "Dark color, I think. Nice suit, as I remember. Handsome."

"You are absolutely sure of your identification?" Sir Alan asked.

Drake frowned over the picture once more. "Oh, yes," he said positively. "This is the fellow all right. Saw him on the street two or three times."

"About the time of the murder," said Sir Alan.

Drake nodded. "About that time. Best I can recall."

Sir Alan handed the photograph to Mrs. Roosevelt. It was the picture of Harry Billingham.

"That man again!" exclaimed Mrs. Roosevelt. "The same one who —"

Sir Alan interrupted. "The same Harry Billingham who appeared at Crittenden House, fobbing himself off as an Oxford don. A professional criminal. If he's here now—in Washington, and on this very street—it's for no innocent purpose, you may be sure."

16

A routine was established for Pamela. Each morning, she left her apartment and went by taxi to the town house of the Comtessa Andrea Bianchi, where she worked all day for Mrs. Roosevelt. Tommy Thompson and other staff members delivered paperwork to her, and she typed many letters as well as the final draft of the column. Each evening, she came home to her apartment, ate her dinner, then went up one flight to Alicia Howell's apartment, where she slept, while a police officer spent the night in her apartment. She was guarded twenty-four hours a day. Not everyone cooperating was identically motivated—Captain Kennelly, for example, was not sure she might not try to skip bail—but Mrs. Roosevelt was firm about Pamela's protection. Whoever had a motive to kill Philip Garber, she said, might have a motive to kill Pamela. They had no right to take a chance with Pamela's safety.

Mrs. Roosevelt's own active role in the investigation diminished somewhat during those hot August days. The focus of the investigation was now on two men who could not be found—Gully Balzac and Harry Billingham. Balzac had disappeared. As for Billingham, all that was known about him was that he had come to the United States in June and had not been seen since, except that Alfred Drake insisted he had seen him two or three times on the street outside Pamela's apartment.

In any event, Mrs. Roosevelt was busy. She knew how deeply the President was concerned about developments in Europe, which, although he did not specifically ask for her help, moved her to remain close to the White House and close to events. She played smiling hostess to Secretary Hull, Mr. Stimson, General Marshall, Ambassador Kennedy, and others; and she listened intently to the dinner-table talk. War, it seemed, was quite possible. The difficult international situation demanded more and more of the President's attention, and it demanded hers.

One evening, she was taking a light dinner with Tommy Thompson, both of them having worked late, when Captain Kennelly called.

"Thought you'd want to know. We've found Gully Balzac. Found his body, actually—he's been murdered."

"Murdered? Where?"

"Here in Washington. In a hotel room. I've asked Sir Burton to come see, but I don't think you should come, Mrs. Roosevelt. I can't keep the reporters away."

The next day, at one o'clock, she arrived at the British Embassy for a small private luncheon in honor of Rebecca, Countess of Crittenden. They sat at a round table before a window that overlooked a cool-looking little garden. The ambassador, Lord Lothian, toasted the countess and the First Lady and then excused himself, explaining that the distressing deterioration of the situation in Europe was making burdensome demands on him. He left Sir Rodney Harcourt, the second secretary, to preside.

To Mrs. Roosevelt's surprise, she found Sir Alan Burton there, too. She was surprised because he had made a point of keeping away from the embassy, saying it was necessary to his incognito and that, besides, the Foreign Office and the Home Office had disagreed bitterly on the issue of sending him to the States. He sat to her left and across the table from Sir Rodney.

"You've kept your distance from us, Sir Alan," said the second secretary to the chief inspector.

"You've not seen my name in the newspapers either," said Sir Alan. "I am at pains to remain inconspicuous."

"Oh," said the countess. "Perhaps I made a mistake in asking Sir Rodney to invite you here today."

"Not at all," said Sir Alan. "I have every confidence in Sir Rodney's circumspection."

"We appreciate the cooperation you have given Sir Alan," said Mrs. Roosevelt to the second secretary.

"I'm afraid I'm not aware—" said Sir Rodney.

"The Yard has sent me a few things—some photographs, chiefly—in the diplomatic pouch," said Sir Alan.

"Ah. I see. . . . Well, I . . . uh, I understand there's been another murder linked to the Garber case."

"Ghastly, isn't it?" said the countess after she had taken a sip of the chilled white wine just poured for her by Sir Rodney. "That at so graciously set a table we are moved to discuss another brutal murder."

"It *was* brutal," said Sir Alan. "It was well that you did not come to that hotel last night, Mrs. Roosevelt."

"Yes, but you must tell me every detail," she said. "I read the small account in the newspaper this morning, which of course does not link the death of Gully Balzac to the Garber murder at all. Do you see such a connection, Sir Alan?"

"It would be difficult to say," he replied.

"Anyway," she said. "Tell us what happened."

Sir Alan drew a long breath. "Well," he said. "It's much like what you see at the scene of any murder. The hotel is small and cheap. In fact, I think the word 'squalid' is not too strong a word to apply to it. Such places always *smell* bad, though I don't suppose you would know what I mean."

"Ghastly!" protested the countess.

Sir Alan nodded. "That's another good word for it. The room was on the second floor: a tiny chamber, furnished with a sorry-looking bed, one chair, a bridge lamp, and a wardrobe. From the look of it, I'd guess Balzac had been living there a week or so—ever since he disappeared, in other words."

"But how was he killed?" asked Mrs. Roosevelt.

"Stabbed," said Sir Alan. "In his sleep, one would judge. The bed was quite bloody."

"Oh, ghastly!" exclaimed the countess.

"A second-floor hotel room," mused Mrs. Roosevelt. "Entered how?"

Sir Alan smiled at her and nodded. "Much the same way Pamela's apartment was entered. A crude, simple lock. Picked."

"In the middle of the night?"

"Apparently. The police questioned the room clerk closely. That was to no purpose, however. The hotel could be entered any number of ways—including simply sneaking by that beer-sodden clerk. The occupants of other rooms were—well, I'm sorry, but they were prostitutes who pursued their trade there. Only one other room on the floor was occupied by what you might call a legitimate hotel guest. He was a railroad engineer who said he'd been spending his overnight stays in Washington in that hotel for twenty-five years and was only sorry it wasn't any longer what he called a railroad hotel."

"No one, of course, heard or saw anything, I would suppose," said Sir Rodney.

"Oh, no," said Sir Alan. "No one would admit to ever having seen Balzac in the hall, even on his way to the bathroom or back. It was plain from the litter in his room that he had eaten all his meals there for some days, apparently slipping out to buy bags of sandwiches and scurrying back."

"It's very curious, isn't it," said Mrs. Roosevelt. "I mean, that the police and the F.B.I. couldn't find Mr. Balzac but whoever killed him could, and did."

"We showed pictures of Harry Billingham and Freddy the Melon to the room clerk and the other occupants of the hotel. No one remembered ever having seen them."

Mrs. Roosevelt shook her head. "We supposed Gully Balzac decided to disappear because Betty McDougal's confession made him a suspect in the murder of Philip Garber. Apparently we were wrong about that."

"Director Hoover suggested as much last night," said Sir Alan.

"He was there?"

Sir Alan nodded. "Keeping much in the background, though. He did not want the reporters to see him."

"It seems to me," said Mrs. Roosevelt, "that Betty McDougal has more to tell us."

"I've arranged to question her this afternoon," said Sir Alan. "If you would like to accompany me . . ."

They were crowded into Captain Kennelly's office: Mrs. Roosevelt, Sir Alan Burton, J. Edgar Hoover, the captain, and Betty McDougal. Rain splashed off the windowsill onto the floor, but they kept the window open for the slight coolness of the wet air.

They might also have kept it open against the smell of Betty

McDougal. She stank of sweat, fresh sweat on her body, stale sweat in her gray jail dress, and of cigarette smoke. She sat apprehensive and stiff on a straight chair. Mrs. Roosevelt sat behind Captain Kennelly's desk, and Sir Alan occupied the one additional chair in the little office. The captain and Director Hoover stood, the captain relieving his feet by resting his bottom on the edge of his desk.

"You know about Gully?" Kennelly asked Betty McDougal.

She nodded. "I heard about it." Her voice was low, as if she were afraid someone outside the room would hear.

"Any ideas?" asked Kennelly.

She shook her head.

"Freddy the Melon?" asked Kennelly.

"No—*why?* Why would *he* want to . . . ?"

"Then who?"

Betty McDougal swallowed dryly. "I don't know. I swear I don't know."

"You swear," said Kennelly scornfully. "Does that mean we're supposed to believe what you say this time?"

"Girl facin' what I'm facin' will tell a lie now and again to protect herself as best she can," said Betty righteously. She smiled shyly. "Won't she?"

"You fingered Gully," said Kennelly. "You didn't use the name, but you fingered Freddy. It comes back to you, Betty."

"No," she whispered hoarsely. "Listen. How did Gully know I fingered him? Before you guys could get to him, he took off. Who called him, Kennelly? You know I didn't."

Kennelly turned down the corners of his mouth, tipped his head, and nodded. "You got a point there, honey," he said.

"Sure. Somebody in your crowd—"

"Maybe. But *why?*" asked Kennelly.

Betty McDougal shook her head. "Somebody give me a smoke?"

"If you please, no," said Mrs. Roosevelt. "This room is too close."

Betty McDougal shrugged. "Whatever that means."

"You'll be going back where you can smoke soon enough," said Kennelly. "*Think.* Who could have wanted Gully's hide? And what for?"

She shook her head slowly. "No idea. Maybe—maybe he had some idea himself, come to think of it. Did Gully have a gun in that hotel room?"

Kennelly nodded. "Two of 'em."

"Okay," said Betty, sighing. "Yeah. He started packin' a rod two or three months ago. Never knew him to do it before. Other guys—I mean, other guys in the club that worked for him—they were packin' 'em, too. Gully was kinda nervous. You suppose he had a warning of some kind?"

"Maybe," said Kennelly. "Who could it have been?"

"Not Freddy the Melon," she said. "I can't think of any reason why the big boys would have it against Gully."

"What big boys?" asked Director Hoover.

"The Baltimore big boys," said Betty McDougal. "He worked for them. Why would they have anything against him?"

"What about the Jersey waterfront big boys?" asked Hoover. "Did you ever see any of them around the club?"

"Phil's dad's friends," she said quietly, fearfully. "No, I never knew of anybody like that being around the club." She shrugged. "Of course, I wouldn't know."

"Betty," said Mrs. Roosevelt, "how much business did Gully Balzac *really* do with Philip Garber?"

Betty McDougal tossed her chin high. "When you asked me before, I said not much. Really, he did a lot. More than just to pay off gambling debts. Gully was Phil's fence. But the jewels out of that English job were too hot. Gully was afraid to touch 'em. That big diamond especially—what you call the Raphael. Gully was afraid to touch that. He threatened to break every bone in Phil's body, like I told you. But Phil threatened to break every bone in his, too. Phil Garber was no kid."

"What did he say?" asked Mrs. Roosevelt. "Repeat that conversation for us."

Betty sighed. "I didn't tell you all of it. There was more to it. Gully was putting the heat on Phil to pay what he owed. Phil said he'd brought in more than enough to pay it five times over, and he pulled out the big diamond. 'There,' he said. 'That's worth your whole damned club.' Gully just got mad. 'It's worth my neck,' he said. 'You were a fool to lay hands on that. Take my advice and give it back to Cynthia. It's not worth a nickel in the market.' "

"He was afraid of other stones, you say?" asked Sir Alan.

Betty nodded. "Beautiful diamonds. He took some, but he told Phil he'd picked out the wrong stuff."

"What did that mean?" asked Director Hoover.

"I don't know."

"But Gully helped you buy the Raphael," said Mrs. Roosevelt. "That is inconsistent."

"Only because we figured Cynthia would keep it, wear it. Anyway, she was rich enough to maybe own a big diamond like that, so it wouldn't get much attention. Who could have figured she'd take it to a jeweler to be set when it was still hot as a firecracker, and who could have figured her jeweler would match it right off to the description of a hot diamond?"

"Cynthia knew all this?" asked Mrs. Roosevelt.

Betty nodded. "She was with Phil when he and Gully had a big squabble. She knew what the diamond was. She knew what it was worth, and she knew Phil couldn't unload it. She knew what she was doing when she bought it. The only time she was stupid was when she took it to her local jeweler and asked him to set it in a ring."

"So who killed Phil Garber?" Kennelly asked.

"Honest to God, I don't know," said Betty. She shook her head. "I supposed Gully, but since *he* got it, I'm fresh out of ideas."

"You'd like to go on the street?" Kennelly asked.

"Don't I wish I could? I was scared of Gully, what he'd do if he knew I fingered him, but I got nothin' to be scared of now, not that I know of. I'd love to go on the street. Behind bars is not my idea of a place to spend your life."

"Three years from now, honey," said Kennelly.

She nodded. "Yeah. Three years. I'm not sure but what Gully's not the lucky one."

"I've checked the stenographer," said Kennelly after Betty McDougal was taken back to her cell. "It's not impossible that she was the one, but I don't think she was. So that leaves us." He paused. "I know it wasn't me, so which one of you called Gully and told him Betty had fingered him?"

Captain Kennelly glanced grimly from Mrs. Roosevelt to Sir Alan Burton to Director Hoover.

"I have another question," said Sir Alan. "Who called Gully's killer and told him where to find him?"

"We don't know anybody did," said Kennelly. "There are a thousand ways the killer could have found him."

"Not a thousand," said Sir Alan. "Only a few. Coincidence—Gully was seen by chance and followed. Habit—he had used that hideout before. Likelihood—someone who knew where he was called his killer and told him where to find him."

"Why is that possibility more likely than the others?" asked Hoover.

"It is unlikely that a man can hole up in a tiny room in a decrepit hotel and for a week overcome the temptation to call someone. It's against human nature. I've seen a hundred similar cases. A man in hiding feels an irresistible compulsion to trust *someone*, even if no one but a prostitute. How many fugitives have we apprehended, Director, because they succumbed to that compulsion?"

Hoover nodded wisely. "True," he said.

"So then someone betrayed him," said Mrs. Roosevelt.

Sir Alan inclined his head toward her. "So I would expect," he said soberly.

Mrs. Roosevelt looked into the faces of each of the others. "I do have to believe, Captain Kennelly," she said, "that we waste our time looking at each other. It really is inconceivable to me that one of us called Gully Balzac and told him Betty McDougal had—how do you say?—'fingered' him. You say it was not you, Captain. I know it was not I. And I can't believe it was Director Hoover or Sir Alan Burton."

"It wasn't the stenographer," said Kennelly.

"Well, we are then at a dead end," said Director Hoover impatiently.

"Betty McDougal, Cynthia Dawes," said Kennelly disgustedly. "Liars! I don't know which one is worse, and I don't know if Betty is telling the truth now. We were wrong to agree to the deal for Cynthia. She belongs in jail."

"There remain," said Sir Alan calmly, "two facts that stand incontrovertible with or without the testimony of those two young women. One is that Gully Balzac fled into hiding within hours after both Betty and Cynthia accused him of hiring someone to kill Philip Garber. The second is that someone found him in his hidey-hole and put him to death, which was no mean feat. I should like to know who called Gully and warned him. Then I should like to know who betrayed him to his killer. When we know that, I suspect we will know our killer."

"How do you propose to find out?" asked Captain Kennelly.

"Oh, I hope a little hard work of the elementary sort will help," said Sir Alan. "If it doesn't, we are, as the director suggests, at a dead end."

17

Her brief midmorning press conference having concluded about eleven, Mrs. Roosevelt remained in the Monroe Room and received Sir Alan Burton, Director Hoover, and Captain Kennelly there. Tommy Thompson brought her her considerable file of notes and other papers relating to the Garber murder and now the murder of Guglielmo Balzac. Mrs. Roosevelt sat with her back to the fireplace, which on this summer day was cold and decorated with a spray of yellow flowers, and the three men sat at the other three sides of the room's small conference table.

"We seem," she said, "to constitute a committee to solve these crimes. I want you gentlemen to know how grateful I am to you for including a rank amateur in your professional efforts. You have been most patient."

"I am sure *we* are all grateful to *you*," said Sir Alan.

"Sir Burton speaks for me," said Captain Kennelly. "If it hadn't been for you, Mrs. Roosevelt, I guess we'd have sent that English girl to the electric chair without much thought or ceremony. It seemed so obvious."

"Yes, uh, I am happy to have had the opportunity to work with you," said Director Hoover.

Mrs. Roosevelt beamed her famous warm smile at them. "Thank you all," she said. Then she sighed, though she was still smiling. "I am afraid it is a little early for us to be feeling self-congratulatory, though. I feel as though I've been working at a Chinese puzzle. Each step forward puts us two paces back."

"I've done some checking about the disappearance of Gully Balzac," said Hoover. "I sent two agents out to the Kit Kat Club to ask some questions. Balzac cleaned out his safe and disappeared within an hour and a half after we concluded our meeting at the Mayflower Hotel. No one knows if he got a phone call. He just suddenly took off, without saying anything. If they are telling the truth, they never heard from him again. It's no coincidence that he picked that particular afternoon to go on the lam."

"I have been working on that problem a little myself," said Mrs. Roosevelt. "Forgive me, but I believe the correct procedure is to follow a logical process of elimination. Will you follow me through this?"

The others nodded.

"Very well. First, then, let us eliminate the four of us. None of us, I feel certain, called Gully Balzac and warned him he had become a principal suspect in the murder of Philip Garber. Captain Kennelly is confident the stenographer did not call. He knows Betty McDougal had no opportunity to call."

"I made sure of that," said Kennelly.

"Well, then, the warning was given by no one who was in the room when Betty McDougal 'fingered' Gully Balzac," said Mrs. Roosevelt.

"Then how could anyone . . ." asked Captain Kennelly.

"If the warning was not given by anyone who was in the room," said Mrs. Roosevelt, "then it had to be given by someone who was not in the room. The question then becomes: how did someone who was not in the room learn Gully Balzac had become a chief suspect?"

"Betty McDougal had fingered Balzac the day before," said Hoover accusingly to Kennelly. "It was known at D.C. police headquarters for twenty-four hours before our meeting at the Mayflower."

"It was known to me only," said Kennelly emphatically.

"You're sure of that?"

"Unless she talked about it back in the cell range," said Kennelly.

"Please excuse me," said Mrs. Roosevelt. "I would like to suggest that one other person knew Betty McDougal had . . . accused Gully Balzac."

"Who?" asked Kennelly.

"Cynthia Dawes," said Mrs. Roosevelt. "You were so kind as to provide me with this copy of the transcript of our meeting, typed up by the stenographic service. If you review the questioning of Cynthia Dawes, you'll see she could easily have understood, from what she was asked, that Gully Balzac had been, as you say, 'fingered' by Betty McDougal. Indeed, she was more than a little accusatory, herself."

"I wondered why Cynthia Dawes was included in that meeting in the first place," said the F.B.I. director.

"Because Betty said Cynthia had overheard Gully threatening Phil," said Kennelly. "I wanted to see if Cynthia would corroborate Betty's statement."

"Anyway," said Mrs. Roosevelt, "Cynthia Dawes probably understood that Gully Balzac had been accused, was now a principal suspect, and might be arrested shortly. Maybe she called him. She was allowed to make any telephone calls she wanted from the Fairfax County jail. Her father's local influence was enough, during the last few days she was there, to win her many privileges not given other prisoners. Restaurants delivered fine meals—with cocktails and wine —to her cell. Or so I'm told."

"Did she make a phone call when she was brought back after our meeting at the Mayflower?" asked Hoover.

"Not just one call," said Mrs. Roosevelt. "Many. I could not, without being quite conspicuous, learn whom she called. I am sure an inquiry, from the D.C. police or the F.B.I., to the telephone company will produce the information we need."

"I can have that information in a minute," said Hoover. "Let me make a call."

He required less than five minutes to learn that a call had indeed been placed from the telephone in the Fairfax County jail to the Kit Kat Club in Maryland within an hour after the conclusion of the meeting at the Mayflower Hotel.

"*I want that girl,*" Hoover growled angrily when he returned to the table. "I'm putting out a federal warrant for her."

"On what charge?" asked Captain Kennelly.

"Charge?" snorted Hoover. "Walking on the grass at the Lincoln Memorial. I don't care what charge. I'm going to have her."

He did have her, before the day was over. Arrested by his agents at her home in Virginia, Cynthia Dawes was locked in a cell in the District jail by four that afternoon. At seven she confronted Hoover, Captain Kennelly, Sir Alan Burton, and Mrs. Roosevelt, in Captain Kennelly's little office.

"You got no *right,* " she sobbed. "My daddy told me you got no right. You got no right a 'tawl t' do this. He said to jus' hold on, he'd get me a writ of habeas corpus in no time."

"Suppose we charge you with being an accessory to the murder of Guglielmo Balzac," said Director Hoover. "Where's your daddy's writ then?"

"I want a lawyer," she said. She tried to smooth the wrinkled skirt of her gray uniform. "I got a right."

"You have a right," Hoover agreed. "Let's see . . . forty-five hours from now, you have a right to see your daddy and see a lawyer. In the meantime, I want to know who killed Philip Garber and who killed Gully Balzac."

"How would I know?" she shrieked.

Director Hoover's chest swelled as he took a deep breath. "Within an hour after you gave us a statement at the Mayflower Hotel, you got on the telephone back at the Fairfax County jail and called Gully Balzac," he said impatiently. "Why? What did you tell him?"

"I *never!*"

"We know you did," said Hoover.

Cynthia Dawes inhaled deeply, then let the air out slowly, slackening as she exhaled. "I had nothin' to do with killin' him," she said quietly, hoarsely. "Nothin'. Absolutely nothin'."

"Why did you call him?" Hoover demanded grimly.

The girl looked for a moment at Mrs. Roosevelt, as if she remembered how Mrs. Roosevelt had joined her demand to have the handcuffs taken off her at the hotel meeting, as if she hoped for some support from her. She blinked out tears.

"Why?" Hoover repeated.

Cynthia sighed. "Gully was fair to me," she said softly. "He told me I'd been cheated worse by Phil than he had been. It's the truth. Phil cheated us all. Gully. Me. Pamela Rush-Hodgeborne. Everybody. He said Phil took advantage of bein' the son of a congressman, took advantage of his daddy's connections with rough people in N' Jersey. I went back to the club to pick up my diamond—I mean *the* diamond —the one I'd bought back. Gully told me that Phil had . . . well, he'd done with Betty McDougal the same as he'd done with Pamela and me. I was feelin' bad. Gully was nice to me. He was a tough kind of man, but he was real nice to me. I never believed he hurt Phil.

When I figured out y'awl thought maybe he was the murderer, I did, I called him, and warned him. Y' wanna send me off to prison for that, Mr. Hoover? That what y' want to do?"

"Gully Balzac was wanted as a suspect in a brutal murder," said Hoover. "You gave him a warning, so he could run away. That's a crime, in case you want to argue you didn't know."

"Cynthia," said Mrs. Roosevelt. "A witness has identified you as a young woman who hung around Pamela's apartment building. What were you doing?"

Cynthia sobbed. "I thought I was gonna marry Phil," she whispered. "I found out he was seein' Pamela also. I wanted to see what kind of girl she was."

"Who killed Gully?" asked Captain Kennelly.

"I swear I don't know!"

"Suppose I tell you," said Kennelly, "that the room clerk at the fleabag hotel where Gully died has identified you from your picture as the girl who visited Gully in his room. What were you doing there?"

"I went to take him food, that's all!" Cynthia cried. "Just went to help him out a little bit, that's all."

Kennelly smiled coldly. "The room clerk didn't identify you," he said. "He just looked at your picture and shook his head. But now that you've told us you went there, tell us how you knew where Gully was."

Cynthia covered her face with her hands. "How much trouble am I in?" she asked, weeping.

Kennelly glanced at Hoover. "We don't really care about you, Cynthia," he said. "We want to know who stole the diamonds from that country house in England, who killed Phil Garber, and who killed Gully Balzac. So talk."

"I don't know!" She wept. "I really don't know! Phil stole the diamonds, I suppose. I don't know who killed him. I don't know who killed Gully."

"How many times did you go to the hotel?"

"Three times. He was afraid to leave his room, so I went and took him food, three times."

"How did you know where he was?"

"He called me. He said he read in the newspaper that I'd been let out of jail, so he called me at home."

"What was he hiding from?" asked Hoover.

She glanced at him. "From you. From all of you. He knew you supposed he murdered Phil."

"Cynthia," said Mrs. Roosevelt. "I believe you've given us two versions now of your meeting with Congressman Frank Garber, after Philip was murdered. Do you want to tell us what he *really* said to you?"

The girl wiped her eyes on the back of her hand. "He wanted to know who killed his son," she said in a low, tearful voice. She drew a breath and sighed. "He wanted to know how much money Phil had owed Gully and if Gully had threatened to kill him. He had his suspicions of Gully, from the first."

"What did you tell him?" asked Mrs. Roosevelt.

"Nothin'," said Cynthia.

"Really? Nothing?"

Cynthia shook her head. "Nothin'. I didn't want to get mixed up in it."

"Is that the truth?" asked Hoover.

Cynthia nodded.

"Gully had two pistols in his room," said Kennelly. "Did he intend to shoot it out with the police?"

Cynthia shrugged disconsolately.

Director Hoover spoke. "He emptied his office safe before he left the Kit Kat Club and fled to that hotel. He must have had a lot of money in his room. What do you know about that?"

She shook her head. "Nothin'. I swear . . ."

"What did he talk about when you were with him?"

She lifted her chin. "He said he was gonna get Betty McDougal if it was th' last thing he ever did."

"For fingering him?"

She nodded.

"There's something I don't understand," said Kennelly. "You came over to Washington from Virginia, went to that dirty old hotel, met with Gully, went out and bought him food . . ."

"And a bottle of whiskey each time," she said. "He asked me to bring him a quart each time."

"Okay. Three times. Why, Cynthia? Don't tell us it was because he was nice to you. What was there between you and Gully Balzac?"

She shook her head. "Nothin'. Absolutely nothin'."

"I don't think any of us are prepared to believe that, dear," said Mrs. Roosevelt softly.

"There was nothin'," said Cynthia again, this time with a note of desperation in her voice.

"How much money did *you* owe Gully?" asked Kennelly.

"None. I didn't owe him nothin'."

"Gambling," said Sir Alan. "You can lose a lot of money gambling, can't you? You told us about the way Philip Garber lost money gambling. It was a lesson you had learned and learned a hard way, wasn't it, Cynthia? I watched you gamble one night, over in Virginia. You lose even more when you *drink* and gamble. Don't you? You can lose a lot that way."

"This isn't fair," Cynthia protested. "Y'awl shootin' questions at me, all at once."

"I wonder," said Sir Alan, "what would happen if we showed your picture to a lot of jewelers, here and in Virginia, maybe in Baltimore and Philadelphia."

"What for?" she asked.

"Oh, just to see how many had bought old family heirlooms from you," said Sir Alan.

Cynthia shook her head. "You're wrong!" she cried.

"Am I?"

Cynthia covered her face with both hands and began to sob. "How much do you know?"

"It would be better if you tell us," said Sir Alan. He shot a cautionary glance into the faces of the others.

With her face still covered, Cynthia sobbed out her response. "Just one time," she insisted. "Just one time. He bought up my markers. He bought up what markers I had out at other places, and he had the ones I'd left with him. They came to six thousand. I could've paid it, but he gave me a chance to pay off without goin' into the property my grandmama left me. Gully had some stuff, what he called merchandise. It wasn't unset diamonds like what Phil had. It was jewelry, like watches and rings and brooches and things like that. He said I could sell stuff like that easy, 'cause it'd be taken for family stuff if I brought it in. I did it. I sold some in Washin'ton, some in Virginia, some in Maryland. I could use my name, you know. Some of the jewelers checked up, to see who I was." She sighed heavily. "I sold almost twenty thousand dollars' worth of stuff, never more than two or three thousand to one jeweler. I even sold one pretty gold watch, set with diamonds, to a friend of mine. I got five hundred for it. Gully paid me half of whatever I could get above a certain price he had set. I paid him off that way, and he tore up my markers. I never gambled in his club again, except for cash I had on me. I'd learned my lesson."

Sir Alan nodded. "Of course," he said. "A perfect arrangement for a fence. They all like to have a respectable citizen or two on the hook. She could sell to honest jewelers, who would suppose she really was selling from her inheritance."

"He told me to say I was short of money," Cynthia said between sobs.

"Then of course he blackmailed you," said Director Hoover.

She drew down her hands, showing her red, tear-streaked face. "He tried," she sobbed. "He wanted me to take Phil's diamonds and sell them the same way." She shook her head. "I wouldn't. I was afraid."

"And you warned him he might soon be arrested in the Garber murder because you were afraid how much he might confess," said Sir Alan. "It was not because you had any affection or respect for him but because you were afraid he might tell the D.C. police or the F.B.I. how you helped him fence stolen jewelry."

She covered her face again, nodded, and began to sob uncontrollably. "He'd have gone crazy if he'd been arrested for murder."

"In fact," said Kennelly harshly, "you fingered him for his killer for the same reason."

"*No!*" she screamed. "I've got nothin' to do with his gettin' killed! Or with Phil's gettin' killed either."

"Who killed him, Cynthia?" Kennelly demanded.

"*I don't know!*" she shrieked.

"It is very difficult, Cynthia," said Mrs. Roosevelt gravely, "to believe someone who has so consistently lied as you have."

Cynthia bent forward, still weeping. "I don't know who killed either one of them. *I don't know!*"

"Cynthia," said Sir Alan in a calm, soothing voice. "I am prepared for the moment to assume that is true. I will ask you, therefore, for some further cooperation. Please look at these photographs and tell us who these people are."

He handed her the photographs one at a time, and she peered at them through her fingers and whispered through her sobs.

The first picture he showed her was of James O'Neill, Mayfair Jimmy. She shook her head and whispered that she had never seen him. The second picture was of Frederick Moellenkopf, Freddy the Melon. She swore she had never seen him. The third was of Harry Billingham.

"Oh," she whispered. "Oh, yes. That's Mr. Rush-Hodgeborne. That's Pamela's daddy."

18

With all four of her questioners staring at her silent and open-mouthed, Cynthia sniffed, looked at the picture of Harry Billingham again, and said, "Well, it *is*. That's Pamela's daddy."

Sir Alan's face was dark red as he glanced at each of the others, then demanded angrily, *"How do you come to know him?"*

"He came to see me. At home. It was just after I got out of the Fairfax County jail. He came to see if I knew anything that could help his little girl, as he said. He's a fine gentleman. I felt sorry for him."

Sir Alan closed his eyes and seemed to fight to regain his composure. "Billingham," he muttered.

"No wonder you lie so badly, Cynthia," said Hoover. "You're too stupid to keep track of your lies."

"I'm *not* lyin'," she protested indignantly. "He—"

Sir Alan opened his eyes and regarded her with rigid anger. "We want you to tell us exactly when and where you saw this man, plus exactly what he said. Your help with this may have a great deal to do with what happens to you. Isn't that right, Director? Captain?"

Hoover and Kennelly nodded soberly.

Cynthia snatched the picture off the corner of the desk and frowned at it a third time. "Who is he?" she asked.

"We'll talk about that later," said Sir Alan.

She tossed the picture back to Kennelly's desk. "Well," she said, "he came to our house. It was in the afternoon. My mama was there and met him, thought well of him. He was a soft-talkin', mannerly kind of man. He said he was a schoolteacher in England and had come to the States to try and help his daughter Pamela. Said he was

tryin' to find out all he could about the case. Said he hoped I wouldn'
mind talkin' to him. He was real polite."

"How did he come to your house?" asked Sir Alan. "Was he driving
a car?"

"Yes. Said he'd rented it and talked about how expensive it was to
rent a car. He said it was takin' just about all his life's savin's to come
to this country and try to help his daughter, but it was somethin' he
had to do."

"Why did he come to see you?"

She paused. "He said he knew Phil had taken advantage of his
daughter and he supposed he'd taken advantage of me the same way.
He said Phil had got his daughter involved in the big burglary in
England, and he'd read in the papers about how I was in trouble for
havin' the Raphael diamond in my possession. He wanted to know
how I'd come to have the diamond. I told him I'd bought it from
Betty McDougal. He said he wanted to see her, but I told him she was
in the jail in Washin'ton. He asked me a lot of questions about her. He
said he figured Pamela had carried lots of stolen diamonds to the
States for Phil, and he wanted to know where all those diamonds
were. He said he thought it would help Pamela if as many as possible
of the stolen diamonds were turned over to the police and got back to
their owner in England."

"And what did you tell him about the whereabouts of the diamonds?" asked Sir Alan.

"I told him the diamonds had been too hot to fence. I mean, that's
what Gully had said about 'em. So then he wanted to know where
they were. Who had 'em? I said I didn't know. He said he supposed
he ought to talk to Gully, and he asked me where Gully was. I said I
didn't know."

"But you did," said Kennelly.

"Yes, I did. But I wasn't tellin' anybody."

"Then what did he say?"

"Nothin' much more. Pretty soon he left."

"Did you ever see him again?"

She shook her head firmly. "No. Never again. I swear."

"I don't suppose," said Hoover, "you by any chance noticed the
license number of his car."

"No," she said. "I most sincerely didn't."

"What kind of car was it?" asked Kennelly.

"A Ford," she said. "Little blue Ford coupe."

Cynthia was returned to her cell, and they waited for Betty McDougal to be brought from hers.

"Billingham," murmured Sir Alan, shaking his head. "I should have known—I *did* know, in fact. That's why I've been showing his picture to everyone."

Kennelly sighed. "Obviously, Cynthia *did* tell him where Gully was holed up. She's lying about that. Afraid we'll charge her as an accessory in Gully's murder."

"This man Billingham is capable of having killed Philip Garber, I suppose," said Mrs. Roosevelt. She had been somewhat surprised at the chief inspector's emotional reaction to Cynthia's identification of Harry Billingham, and she was watching him regain his calm. "I mean, his record—"

"Oh, capable, you may be sure," said Sir Alan. "God grant me that I hang him this time! He's escaped too often."

When Betty McDougal was brought in, Sir Alan handed her the photograph of Billingham and drew up indignantly, waiting for her response. "Never saw the man," she said with a shrug.

"Really," said the chief inspector coldly. "Then I should like, Miss McDougal, for you to be very specific about the jewels Gully Balzac considered too hot to fence. How many did Philip have? And what became of them?"

Betty McDougal rubbed her eyes. She looked as though she had been asleep. "I don't know how many he had," she said. "A few. Maybe a dozen. Maybe twenty."

"All unmounted diamonds?"

"A couple of the bigger stones were emeralds. Beautiful!"

"He brought them in over a period of time?"

She nodded. "He kept tryin' to get Gully to take them as payment for what he owed—or for cash. He always needed cash. Gully did take a few small ones. But the big ones . . . Gully was scared to death of them."

"There was more than one in the jar of cream, apparently," mused Mrs. Roosevelt.

"What did he do with them, then?" asked Sir Alan. "Where are they now?"

Betty shrugged. "Beats me. He was peddling them off here and there, one at a time, getting much less than he should have. I don't know if he had any left when—"

"Why do you suppose," asked Mrs. Roosevelt, "he gave the Raphael diamond to Cynthia Dawes?"

Betty shook her head. "Maybe it was a good way to hide it," she said. "He must have known he could get it back from her. Or maybe it was an investment. He couldn't sell it, so he used it to set up a marriage with her, to get at her money. I wouldn't put that past him."

Captain Kennelly lifted one foot to the windowsill and retied his shoe. "You're facing three years, Betty," he said. "How'd you like to cut a year or two off?"

She sighed loudly. "You know the answer, Kennelly. I'd strangle my grandmother for a passport out of stir."

"Then tell us where we can find some of those jewels. *Any* of them. Give us a good guess if you don't know. You can buy yourself some time off."

"Jeez, I wish I could," she said unhappily. "Try anyplace where he gambled. Try Peter McIntosh at that spiffy club over in Virginia. Try Washington loan sharks."

"No original ideas, huh?"

She shook her head. "Sorry, Kennelly. You don't know how sorry I am."

Ordinarily, Mrs. Roosevelt avoided the President's cocktail hour in the sitting room on the second floor. It was, somehow, Franklin's special time, when he escaped into something his own of which she did not especially want to be a part—of which, she had understood for a long time, *he* did not especially want her to be a part. Ordinarily, she did not very much enjoy the people who gathered around him then, or their conversation. When she was there, they did not speak as freely as they might otherwise have done. To stay away was better judgment.

This evening she made an exception. She sat down on the sofa with Harry Hopkins. Arthur grinned and went off to fetch her some tea.

"I hope you don't mind talking about Pamela's matter a bit," she said when the President had mixed his martinis and her pot of tea was before her. She poured tea and savored the scented steam. "It's coming to a head."

"If Harry will promise not to suggest that Philip Garber was murdered by the GPU or the Gestapo, it will be a relief to talk about your murder mystery, Babs," said the President.

She spoke for a few minutes, filling them in on what she had learned in the last day or two.

"Billingham," said Missy. "It all comes round to Billingham, apparently."

"Analyze logically," suggested Hopkins. "What was *his* motive for killing Garber?"

The President smiled and rubbed his hands together. "Logically," he said, nodding. "Motive number one, he wanted revenge. Simple falling-out among thieves. Philip cheated his partners in crime, so they sent a man to kill him."

"But Philip Garber has been dead for some time," Hopkins objected. "Why would Miss—uh, Dawes, is it? Why would Miss Dawes see Billingham in Virginia so long after—"

"Which is exactly the question I've asked," interrupted Mrs. Roosevelt. "I think you're right, Harry. I don't think revenge is the motive."

"*Second,* I was about to say," the President continued, raising two fingers. "Second, Billingham thought many valuable jewels were still in Philip's possession. He meant to get them."

Mrs. Roosevelt nodded. "We know the girl's lapel watch was full of diamonds. We know one large diamond, the Raphael, came into this country in a jar of face cream. It's very likely others were in the face cream, pressed down to the bottom of the jar the night of the Austin House burglary. Philip knew how sparingly Pamela used her lavender-scented cream. He knew he had months in which to recover any jewels in the bottom of the jar."

"Tens of thousands of dollars' worth," marveled Missy.

"Yes," said Mrs. Roosevelt. "As much as a million dollars' worth remains unrecovered."

"Then Billingham killed Gully Balzac, I suppose," said the President. "He believed Balzac had the jewels."

"Had taken them as Philip's fence," agreed Hopkins.

"All of which means," said Mrs. Roosevelt, "that Pamela is in constant danger. So long as an immense fortune in jewels remains unaccounted for, the people who stole them—specifically this man Billingham, but probably others equally dangerous—will suspect *she* has them and might kill her in the effort to get their hands on them."

"She is under guard, is she not?" asked the President.

"As a matter of fact," said Mrs. Roosevelt, "she sleeps in another apartment, and a police officer keeps watch all night, every night, in hers."

The President sipped from his martini. "I can see this case dragging on into 1943," he said. "Could we agree to be precipitous?"

"We got where we are being that way," said Mrs. Roosevelt. "What do you have in mind, Franklin?"

The President leaned back in his wheelchair and stared for a brief moment at the ceiling. "Be sure the girl is well guarded, Babs. Call on me if you have to, to see she is well and thoroughly protected. Then let's bait a trap."

"How?" asked Mrs. Roosevelt.

The President reached for his cigarette holder and frowned distastefully at a cigarette he had allowed to go out. "Harry," he said, "if among us we can't plant a newspaper story, then we ought not to be in this business. . . ."

The next day, looking at identical stories in the *Post* and the *Star*, Mrs. Roosevelt smiled at Harry Hopkins and said, "Look. Steve Early merits a medal. What a talent for bamboozling the press! Both of them ran it!"

The small news item read:

> A diamond turned over to police yesterday by the proprietor of a small Georgetown jewelry store has been identified as a part of the loot taken in last winter's notorious Austin House burglary in England. The jeweler told police he became suspicious when a young woman who came in with the precious stone grew conspicuously nervous as he was appraising it. When he told her he would have to make a telephone call or two before he could make her an

offer for the diamond, she became frightened and ran from the store, leaving the diamond behind, he said.

Elihu Marx, the jeweler, described the young woman as pretty, blond, and about twenty-one years old. The diamond was appraised by Marx as having a value of at least one thousand dollars.

The evening of the next day, Mrs. Roosevelt had dinner in Alicia Howell's apartment, with Alicia, Pamela, and Rebecca, Countess of Crittenden. Mrs. Roosevelt was keeping an appointment she had made a week before, even though the situation in Europe this last week in August had so far deteriorated that she felt some obligation to stay at the White House. So much did she feel the tug of two obligations, the one to appear at the dinner that was so important to her two friends Alicia and Pamela, the other to be at the President's side in the event of an international crisis, that she allowed the Secret Service to install a special telephone line from the White House to the Howell apartment for the evening.

With a book of paper matches, Alicia Howell lighted the candles on her dining table. "Whoever thought," she said breathlessly, "I'd someday be serving dinner to the First Lady and a British countess? Pour the wine, will you, Pamela?"

Pamela poured white wine into four red glasses.

"How very delightful!" said Mrs. Roosevelt as she was seated.

"My husband, Captain Howell, brought the candle holders back from Samoa," said Alicia Howell. "Supposed to be human bones."

"Let us pretend they're pig bones," said Pamela.

"The wine . . . ?" asked the countess apprehensively.

"Rhine wine. Bought it at the wineshop this afternoon."

"Ah," said the countess, relieved.

Mrs. Roosevelt and the countess were dressed for dinner in floor-length gowns: Mrs. Roosevelt's blue silk, the countess's white. The countess wore a necklace of diamonds and emeralds. Alicia Howell wore red and white, and remarked that her dress matched her table setting. Pamela wore a simple white blouse, a tailored black skirt, and black patent-leather shoes. She wore no makeup to lend color to her pale face.

"Who is on duty downstairs?" asked Pamela, betraying her thoughts.

"A District detective," said Mrs. Roosevelt. "Sir Alan himself will relieve him later. Sir Alan is dining at the embassy but will come here as soon as he can."

"I hope those newspaper stories produce some result soon," said Pamela. "It makes me nervous."

"This is only the second night since they appeared," said Mrs. Roosevelt. "We must be patient, they tell me."

"Patience is a luxury for people only tangentially involved in something," said Pamela. "When you are personally involved, it is not so easy."

"Well, anyway, you are here," said Alicia Howell cheerfully. "Out of jail . . ."

"But not out of trouble," said Pamela.

While both Alicia and Pamela were in the kitchen, putting coffee and dessert on a tray, the White House line rang. Mrs. Roosevelt hurried to pick it up, dreading what news it might bring.

"One moment for Director Hoover," said the operator.

"Mrs. Roosevelt!" came the booming, enthusiastic voice of the director of the Federal Bureau of Investigation. "Great good news! My fellows have picked up Freddy the Melon!"

"Oh . . . where?" she asked.

"In San Francisco."

"Well. If he's in San Francisco, he's unlikely to be the man who killed Gully Balzac, don't you think?"

"Unless he flew out there!" said Hoover, laughing, his enthusiasm undiminished.

"Yes. Well, I suppose he could have done that."

"I'm flying out there myself. I want to question Freddy the Melon *in person.*"

"Well, why not?" she said. "We're doing nothing much here."

"Yes, good, good! Okay. Well, I'm giving an interview or two here at the airport, and there are some fellows waiting to take pictures of me boarding the plane. I'll be bringing Freddy back!"

"Wonderful," she said dryly.

"Thank you. See you in a few days."

"Yes. Good-bye."

Over coffee and dessert, Pamela and the countess talked about happy times in London and in the country, about the English summer Pamela had missed by being in the States, part of the time in jail.

"We will go to the Riviera for a holiday," said the countess, "if you can come home before the weather turns nasty."

Alicia Howell's telephone rang. She answered and after a moment turned to Mrs. Roosevelt and Pamela, flushed and frowning. "That was Captain Kennelly," she said. "He's on his way here—said he'd be here in a few minutes; but in the meantime, he said, we're not to open the apartment door for anyone."

"That sounds ominous," said Mrs. Roosevelt. "But . . . there are guards on duty in the hallway and all around the building: Secret Service and D.C. police as well. I am sure we are safe."

"Scary, though," said Alicia Howell.

"Yes," said the countess. "One can't help but be frightened."

"Please," said Mrs. Roosevelt firmly. "Let's continue with our dessert and coffee."

"I hope," murmured the countess distractedly, "that Herr Hitler will defer whatever ghastly work he is planning until we have had our holiday."

Captain Kennelly knocked on the door and spoke so they could be reassured by his voice. Alicia Howell admitted him to her apartment.

"I'm sorry if I scared you," said Kennelly, standing just inside the door and facing the four silent, staring women. "It's come too close for comfort."

"Specifically, please," said Mrs. Roosevelt thinly.

"In the alley out back," said Kennelly. "Just behind the building. Billingham. And he's dead. Strangled."

"Billingham!" exclaimed the countess. "We've been sitting here terrified he might at any moment come through a window, and . . . what a relief!"

"Not at all, Rebecca," said Mrs. Roosevelt. "Someone has killed three men—Philip, Balzac, and now Billingham—and we are left without a suspect."

"I've put two men in the hall, right outside your door," said Captain Kennelly. "So don't be afraid. But don't go out, either. Unless—unless, that is, Mrs. Roosevelt, you want to go back to the White House."

She shook her head. "Not for the moment," she said. "I want to stay here at least until Sir Alan comes."

"Right," said Kennelly. "Well . . . my respects. I'll be back shortly."

As he left, he held the door open for a moment and let them see the two uniformed officers standing outside. A Secret Service man sat on the nearby stairs and rose stiffly, as if to stand at attention, when he saw Mrs. Roosevelt regarding him curiously. Kennelly closed the door.

The countess had left the table and now sat heavily slumped on the sofa. Her face was scarlet, and she kept shaking her head.

"Are you all right?" Alicia Howell asked solicitously. "Would you like a little whiskey?"

The countess shook her head. "My glass of wine," she whispered.

Mrs. Roosevelt reached for the special White House telephone. "I'm going to call the British Embassy," she said. "Sir Alan must not linger over dinner tonight."

Nervously busying herself, Pamela helped Alicia Howell clear the table, while the First Lady spoke to the White House operator and ordered a call put through to Sir Rodney Harcourt. The call took some time to complete. Sir Rodney had to be called from his dinner, the embassy operator explained.

"Ah, Mrs. Rose-vult," the familiar voice said finally. "Harcourt here. What can I do for you?"

"Has Sir Alan left the embassy?" she asked anxiously.

"He's not been here, ma'am. Why would you suppose the man is here?"

She paused. "Uh, is Sir Alan not having dinner at the embassy?"

Sir Rodney sighed loudly. "Mrs. Rose-vult . . ." he said. "I . . . uh, have tried to call you several times this evening, but the White House has said you are not available. I would have called even sooner, but I wanted to be reasonably certain of my facts before I did something potentially foolish. I *do* have the facts now. And . . ." He sighed again. "Well, Mrs. Rose-vult, I must tell you that Chief Inspector Sir Alan Burton probably had his dinner at the Beefsteak and is now comfortably sleeping in his quarters in Kensington. He returned to London from his mission to Stockholm more than a week ago and has not been away from London since."

"But . . . ?"

"An impostor, I'm afraid. He aroused my suspicion when he said he had received those photographs from London in the diplomatic pouch. That seemed irregular, so I inquired. He had in fact received nothing. So I cabled London. The Foreign Office did not much expedite my inquiry, but the answer came late this afternoon. Scotland Yard has no idea who this man is. Indeed, they would quite like to know."

"But I thought you *vouched* for the man, Sir Rodney!" Mrs. Roosevelt protested.

"I didn't, ma'am, actually. Even so, he showed us impeccable credentials when he arrived here. Documents . . . they *looked* genuine. Indeed, perhaps they *were* genuine—and stolen."

Even as she listened to Sir Rodney Harcourt, who now continued to say that the imposter might be dangerous and that she should be guarded from him, the door opened, and the man she knew as Sir Alan Burton entered the apartment. He smiled warmly, but as the door closed behind him he drew a small, ugly revolver from inside his coat, put a finger to his mouth to demand their silence, and used the revolver to wave the four women to their places around the dining table.

19

He glanced behind him, at the door just closed for him by one of the uniformed policemen guarding the apartment. His smile widened. "They would hardly refuse admittance to a chief inspector from Scotland Yard, now, would they?" He chuckled.

"If you were to fire a shot from that pistol," said Mrs. Roosevelt, "they would break down that door and be in here to subdue—or kill —you in five seconds."

He glanced down at the pistol. "I have no doubt that's what they would try," he said. He shrugged. "But I've got out of worse scrapes. Suppose, for example, I held you in front of me as a shield? Consider also that if I had to fire, one of you would . . . Well, let's not compound the unpleasantness of the situation. What I want to talk about is, where are my gems and how am I to recover them and escape from here, leaving all of you unharmed? That's what I want. How are we going to work that out?"

His voice was changed. Even his manner, his carriage were different. He spoke still in the Oxford-cum-Edinburgh tones that had been so characteristic of him before, but colored now by elements of a London street accent. He had relaxed his erect bearing and stood with his hips and shoulders atilt. He wore a black wool suit.

"We can finish our work, and you can all be home by bedtime," he said as he hooked a chair into position to face them and sat down, holding the pistol pointed at them. "I think it is not very complicated, and what I want is not far from here."

"What is your name?" Mrs. Roosevelt demanded gruffly.

"Mostly I'm called Archie," he said. "Formally, I'm Archibald Adkins, at your service. Ah, don't cry, Mrs. Howell, don't cry. You're not going to be hurt. And neither are you, Mrs. Roosevelt. I have no wish to harm the First Lady."

"You may not be able to pick and choose whom you hurt," she said coldly.

"It's *my* choice, dear lady, not to hurt anyone," said Adkins.

"Indeed?" said Mrs. Roosevelt scornfully. "Except, of course, that you killed Philip Garber, Guglielmo Balzac, and, I suppose, Harry Billingham."

Adkins shrugged. "You can't make an omelette without breaking eggs," he said. "Of course, I didn't do in Gully Balzac. It was Harry as did that. Poor 'Arry. He shouldn't have muddled in."

The countess, with both hands covering her face, wept and shook. "Ohhh," she wailed. "Three men dead!"

Adkins cast her a nervous glance. "I haven't all night," he said. "I propose to take my gems and make my escape. Where are they, Pamela? In your flat somewhere?"

"She doesn't have them, Mr. Adkins," said Mrs. Roosevelt firmly. "Didn't you learn that much, in your role as detective?"

"She *has* got them," growled Adkins. "A hundred thousand pounds' worth maybe. More than half a million in your money. Maybe more. A lot more than that, even, is missing from what we got out of the safe at Austin House. I remind you, ladies, I've killed two men for them. Pamela . . ."

"The newspaper stories were planted by my husband's press office, Mr. Adkins. No blond young woman tried to sell a diamond to the jeweler named Marx. It was a trap, and you have fallen into it—though not, I must admit, in the way we expected."

"It was Harry as fell into the trap, dear lady, not me," said Adkins. "You trapped him for me, for which I'm properly grateful. Myself, I have never doubted from the beginning that Pamela has the gems—or knows where they are. She's a smart girl, dear lady. Smarter than you think."

"Why do you believe I have them?" Pamela protested in a shrill voice. "It was Philip who had them. He—"

"He's dead, which is wot I warned him he would be if he didn't hand over what he took from his mates. While you were engaged in so helpfully pouring him a cyanide cocktail for me, I searched his flat. Thoroughly. I—"

"Did you kill my dog?" Alicia Howell suddenly demanded.

Adkins sighed. "I regret that very much, Mrs. Howell," he said. "My arse regrets it, too, I may tell you. Your little doggy had sharp teeth and more nearly frustrated me in my purposes than any human adversary I've encountered."

"But—why did you come to my apartment in the first place?"

"I'd just arrived in the States. My first visit. I didn't realize that in this peculiar country the ground floor of a building is numbered as the first story, the first story is numbered as the second story, and so on. So I confused flats Two-C and Three-C. There are no numbers on your doors, only letters, so I picked the wrong bloody lock."

"Wearing the suit you are now wearing," suggested Mrs. Roosevelt, eyeing his black Scottish wool.

"Yes. But the other pair of trousers," Adkins agreed.

"The bit of fabric on Pamela's sofa . . . ?"

"I put it there," Adkins said, with a smile.

"Why, for heaven's sake?" asked Mrs. Roosevelt.

"I knew the dog had died with a bit of my pants and a little of my blood in his mouth."

"I still don't understand why—"

"Dear lady," he interrupted firmly. "I had to get *that one*"—pointing grimly at Pamela—"out of the clink. At first that was where I wanted her, but when I realized it was Pamela, not Philip, and not the assorted gamblers and tarts he counted for his friends, as had the missing gems, I had to get her out. How else was I to pry the secret out of her? And it worked, too, didn't it? The evidence of that little piece of wool, more than anything else, I'd say, brought Captain Kennelly and Director Hoover around to your point of view—that poor Pamela should be released from durance vile. Rather good show I put on, don't you think?"

"Very clever," said the First Lady.

"In fact—won't you acknowledge?—I brought off the whole thing pretty well. Be sporting of you to acknowledge that."

Mrs. Roosevelt only shook her head.

"Good thing for you, Pamela," he said, "that you had a Scotland Yard man on the case, even if he was a fake. Without my work helping Mrs. Roosevelt, you would be well on your way to the electric chair by now."

"Why do you insist that I have the jewels?" Pamela asked tearfully.

"Well, who else could, dear? We know what was in that old safe of the earl's. A friend of ours at the assurance society had shown us the inventory. When my crew and I sat down over our tea to take stock of what all our risk and labor had produced, we found we had less than half of what we'd gone after. Somebody had done us a bad turn. Philip, it was. We know it was Philip, of course. He used our burglary to cover his own. He opened the safe before we got there and skimmed off the cream of the collection."

"Then you and Philip had been working together?" asked Mrs. Roosevelt.

Adkins glanced at his watch. "I don't have much more time for talk," he said. Then he shrugged. "I suppose, though, I do owe you a little more of the story, Mrs. R. You're a good old girl and have been very kind. So . . . Once in a lifetime—twice, actually, in my case, since it was yours truly as gathered in the Druzhinsky gems in 1928— a chance comes to lift a really big haul of loot. We knew about the earl's collection. We knew he kept it in an old safe. We knew, too, about his guard dogs and his alarm system. We were studying Austin House, trying to form a plan, when along comes the Garber lad—a godsend, we thought, though he turned out to be too clever by half. He owed some nine hundred pounds' gaming debts in London clubs, and the time was coming when someone was going to start bashing him about. He began to show up at clubs and offer rings and watches and the like, in payment of what he owed. Obviously, he was a second-story man, with some skills and no scruples, even if he was the son of an American congressman. Well . . . What more need I say? I bought up his debts and recruited him. For his part in our operation, he was to be paid five thousand pounds and all his debts canceled."

"How could he have opened the safe?" asked Pamela.

Adkins sighed impatiently. "One of his jobs was to get the name and serial numbers off the safe, so we could get a like one and let our man practice on it. Philip sat and watched him one afternoon and, I imagine, learned the technique. It was an easy lock, actually—no great difficulty. The challenge was to get inside the house in the first place."

The countess stared openmouthed, moaning, her face wet and red.

"Jewels to the value of a million dollars did not come into this country with Pamela in her lapel watch and jar of face cream," said Mrs. Roosevelt. "Surely you don't believe that."

"She came in as a member of the countess's staff," said Adkins. "I doubt her luggage was searched." He shrugged. "Of course, the bulk of the property may be still in England, waiting for her return."

"Maybe Philip hid it and died with the secret," said Mrs. Roosevelt.

"I don't think so. For the rest of his life, he would have been a suspect, watched by the Yard every time he entered England. No, I think he found some way to bring the gems to the States—and that some way is sitting there looking at me, all innocent-eyed. She's a wealthy woman, Mrs. R. Maybe wealthier than the countess."

Pamela shook her head. "No . . . No!"

"Who was Harry Billingham?" asked Mrs. Roosevelt.

Adkins shrugged. "He's the man as opened the safe. He became very angry when he learned his share of the take was less than half of what he'd expected. He would have killed Philip in London if we hadn't stopped him. Then he disappeared, and I was afraid he'd come to the States and was lurking about, watching for his chance to recover the property all on his own. That's why I brought his photo and some others and kept showing them around, to learn if anyone had seen him. The Balzac killing was a sample of Harry's style. We may be quite sure Balzac didn't have the gems, except maybe a few that Philip fenced with him. I recognized Harry's work when I saw Balzac's corpse. Harry questioned him quite severely before he let him die. Balzac couldn't tell him where the gems were. He'd have told him if he could."

Adkins sighed heavily. "You see, one by one, the possibilities have been eliminated. Some greedy little people—Balzac, Betty McDougal, poor little Cynthia Dawes—have got their hands on a gem or two from the collection and schemed to get more. But in the end it comes back to Philip and Pamela. No one else had the opportunity to skim the cream off."

Adkins stood. "Now, ladies," he said menacingly, thrusting the revolver forward. "Mrs. R., Mrs. Howell, Countess. . . . Keep still and quiet. Pamela and I are going to leave. We are going to pass by the guards outside—who still think I'm Sir Alan Burton—and go down to Pamela's flat. There, she's going to give me the jewels. Or if I don't get them there, then she's going to leave the building with me. We—"

"You can't possibly get past Captain Kennelly," said Mrs. Roosevelt.

"Why not? He still thinks I'm what he calls Sir Burton, chief inspector from Scotland Yard. Of course, you three ladies could raise the alarm. But you won't, because if you do, I will shoot Pamela in the back. Come along now, Pamela. Come with me. You are too clever a girl to do anything foolish."

Slowly, very reluctantly, Pamela rose. Her eyes were filled with tears, and her face was colorless.

Rebecca, Countess of Crittenden, abruptly stood up from the sofa, pallid and shaking. "What will you do with the girl if she won't—or can't—tell you where the jewels are?" she asked hoarsely.

Adkins stiffened. "I have means of persuading her," he said.

The countess glanced at Mrs. Roosevelt, then at Pamela. She shook her head. "She *can't* tell you where they are," she whispered. "She doesn't know."

"I think she does," growled Adkins, "and I've wasted enough time." He reached for Pamela's arm. *"Come along now."*

"No!" the countess protested in a shrill whisper. "She doesn't know. She's more innocent than even she herself understands."

With a hard grip on Pamela's arm, Adkins jerked her off balance and shoved her toward the door. "Remember," he said. "Nothing foolish. None of you."

"Adkins!" the countess hissed. "Listen! She doesn't *have* the missing jewels. She has no idea where they are. Because *I* took them. *I* have them, back in England, where you can't touch them."

"You lie!"

"No. Philip Garber was a small-time thief. He cheated you to the extent of a few stones—the ones he smuggled into the States in Pamela's lapel watch and face cream. But he never had the courage to skim off the best of the collection. He only took what he thought you would never miss. You're not stupid, Adkins. You're no bad judge of character. Do you really think Philip Garber had the courage to steal half your loot from under your noses an hour before your long-planned burglary?"

Adkins pushed Pamela aside. "He came to see us after," he muttered, scowling. "Asked for his five thousand pounds . . ."

"Yes," said the countess. "Would he have come to London and faced you if he had just done you out of *two hundred* thousand?"

"I thought he had cheek," muttered Adkins.

"Cheek! He'd have had to be insane. You threatened to kill him."

"You may believe we did."

"All he had stolen were the few stones he put in Pamela's watch and face cream," said the countess. "He had no idea that you'd not gotten half what you came to Austin House for."

Adkins sighed. "So how did *you* get your hands on it all?"

The countess glanced at Mrs. Roosevelt, then dropped heavily onto her chair. "Philip Garber was a very attractive young man when first one met him and had no clues to his character," she said softly. "I met him at a club in London, in the bar, while the earl was at the gaming tables. We became acquainted, and—well, you know." She drew a breath. "He swived me, the same as he did Pamela."

"Oh, My Lady!" cried Pamela.

"I was quite stricken with him," the countess went on. "I needed an excuse for him to come to our house and indeed perhaps for him to come to the country with us, to Austin House. It was I who suggested he contrive to meet Pamela and pretend to court her. He won the friendship of the earl as well. Those weeks he lived with us at Austin House, he must have slept little, what with visiting my bedroom, then Pamela's, and often being up at dawn to go riding with the earl. By the time I realized what sort of young man he actually was, and how I had been deceived, I had already entertained his proposition that I assist him in the burglary."

"Rebecca!" exclaimed Mrs. Roosevelt.

"You may think me a foolish woman, Eleanor, but I had my reasons, and being briefly stricken with a man young enough to be my son was not my only reason."

"But, Rebecca!"

"He told me he was threatened with maiming, perhaps death, if he did not repay certain gaming debts in London clubs. The jewels were insured, he insisted—which I knew they were. He said his own share of the proceeds from the burglary would be forty percent, about two hundred thousand pounds, of which he would give half to me."

The countess stopped, wiped her flushed and sweating face with the back of her hand, and continued: "I needed that money, Eleanor. I had reason to believe—indeed, I still do—that the earl would eventually squander all he owns at the tables, leaving us impoverished. If somehow I could acquire and set aside a substantial share of the value of his collection of unmounted gems—"

"But *Rebecca!* You have defrauded the insurance companies!"

The countess raised her chin. "I suppose I have. Anyway, Adkins, you could not have carried off the burglary without me. The earl kept his collection in an old safe that was secure against no one but the servants, but his alarm system was quite sophisticated, and he kept the disabling key on his person or at his bedside at all times. Philip had been frustrated in his efforts to get at the key. That was why he . . . well, he played on my affection for him and on my sympathy. He told me the things men usually tell women when they wish to take advantage of them, and besides he told me he would be injured or murdered by London underworld persons if he did not help them carry out the burglary."

"He never mentioned you," said Adkins gruffly. He remained standing with his back to the door, the revolver still in his right hand but with the muzzle now pointing at the floor. "He said he could disable the alarm system all right himself."

The countess continued talking as if she had not heard. "I agreed to disable the alarm." She paused. "But a day or so before the burglary was to come off, it occurred to me that Philip had rogered me thoroughly, in every sense. What assurance did I have that he would pay over any share of the proceeds of the crime? How could I complain if he didn't? Yet what would he do if I threatened to withdraw from his scheme? Make it known to the earl that he visited my bedroom at night?"

"Rebecca . . ."

"The safe was entered *three* times that night. I was first. I knew the combination. I removed almost half the collection, including some of the very best pieces. I secured my loot in a secret compartment in the wine cellar, a hiding place that was built into the house in the times of Charles I, where, needless to say, the Scotland Yard operatives failed to find it. Philip was second. He took the jewels he put in Pamela's watch and cream. Finally—"

"Finally came the *real* burglars: poor, innocent, unsuspecting chaps," Adkins interrupted resentfully.

"Yes," said the countess, now calm, with a little triumph in her voice. "You got enough. A good night's work. But you've *killed* for the rest of it."

Adkins again seized Pamela's arm. "We'll discuss it further, little girl," he said to her. "At the very least, you're my shield, for my escape. Once again, ladies—nothing foolish."

Just as he jerked Pamela roughly to him, the telephone rang. It was Alicia Howell's line, not the White House line.

"Answer it," he said gruffly to Alicia. "And be very careful what you say."

Trembling, the terrified woman lifted the handset from its cradle. She listened for a moment. "It's for you," she said to Adkins, holding it toward him.

Adkins took the phone. He stood close to Mrs. Roosevelt, and the voice on the line was so loud she could hear both sides of the conversation.

"Sir Burton?"

"Kennelly?"

"We've been listening through microphones we hid in the apartment before the first night Pamela stayed there. The building is surrounded. Put the gun down, open the door, and come out."

"It seems to me, Kennelly, that I'm still holding a few cards. Let me see . . . I've four queens."

"Well, I've got four aces, mister."

"In this instance, four queens may be the better hand."

"If the slightest harm comes to Mrs. Roosevelt, I swear to you, mister, you won't leave this building alive."

"I have no intention of hurting her. What I want now is to walk out of this building. How shall we arrange it?"

"We won't."

"You had best be reasonable, Captain. As I said, I hold four queens."

"You son of a—"

"Ugghhh!" grunted Adkins. He dropped both telephone and revolver as he clutched at his belly. Staggering, he pulled eight inches

of heavy, curved Moroccan throwing knife out of the bright wet stain that was spreading over his shirt.

Pamela opened the door. Police and Secret Service men pounded in from the hallway. In a moment the apartment was crowded with them, all talking at once. Adkins had fallen to the floor, and two men began to strip away his bloody shirt. Four Secret Service men surrounded Mrs. Roosevelt, guarding her so tightly she could hardly see what was happening.

She almost failed to notice Alicia Howell stoop and pick up the odd-shaped blade Adkins had pulled from his belly. "My late husband brought the pair of these back from Morocco," she explained to no one in particular. "He showed me how to . . . You have to sort of flip your wrist. I mean, *flip*. Like *this*."

The President sat propped up in bed, his pince-nez in place, touching his lighter to the cigarette he had just inserted in his holder. "Pointed a *gun* at you? Actually pointed a revolver at you, Babs? I—"

"That element of the matter will be withheld from the newspapers," she said. "There's no point in stirring up a lot of excitement. In fact, I think we will succeed in withholding most of it."

He shook his head. "I had no idea you were taking such a risk."

She smiled. "Frankly, neither did I."

The President drew smoke from his cigarette and for a long moment was silent, tipping his head to one side and regarding her with a smile that slowly spread across his face. "You want Edgar's job?" he asked with a chuckle. "Sherlock Roosevelt, Director of the Federal Bureau of Investigation?"

"Oh, let's leave it to Mr. Hoover," she said with a grin. "I do better work *unofficially*."

The President nodded, and then his smile faded. "It was a good job of work, Babs. Typical of you. When you get your eye fixed on the *right* of a thing, the justice of it, you never give in till you see your justice done. Even if—"

"Well, you can't just stand aside and let *injustice* prevail!" she protested.

The President laughed. "Of course not," he said. "Of course not. But please, Babs, try in future to avoid adventures with people who point guns. I mean, doesn't life hold enough adventure for you without—"

She interrupted him with a firm squeeze of his hand. "Being married to Franklin Roosevelt is the greatest adventure anyone could ever have," she said quietly.

He leaned forward and kissed her on the cheek. "Thank you," he said. "I've never known anyone I'd rather share it with."

On Friday morning of that week, German forces invaded Poland. Mrs. Roosevelt had gone up to Hyde Park and received the news from the President, who telephoned her from the White House before dawn. What he and she had dreaded, though expected, had come to pass. In the press of events that autumn and through the following years, she almost forgot the adventure of the Austin House burglary and the three murders she had helped to solve.

She took note, however, that:

On February 3, 1940, Archibald Adkins was electrocuted for the murder of Philip Garber.

On September 11, 1940, Cynthia Dawes was released from the federal women's reformatory at Alderson, West Virginia, where she had served a one-year term. It had been arranged for her to plead guilty to one charge of obstructing justice, in return for dismissal of all other charges.

On September 24, 1942, Betty McDougal was released from the Maryland penitentiary, where she had served a three-year term for receiving the stolen Raphael diamond.

On December 8, 1942, Her Ladyship Rebecca, Countess of Crittenden, was granted early release from Holloway Prison, where she was serving a five-year term for having defrauded the insurers of the Crittenden jewels of more than two hundred thousands pounds. Brigadier Sir Reginald Napier, Fifth Earl of Crittenden, had been wounded at El Alamein, and she was allowed to go home to nurse him.

On November 11, 1945, Pamela Rush-Hodgeborne married Flight Officer Richard Spencer, D.S.O., an R.A.F. pilot she had met during her wartime service as a WREN.

By then Mrs. Roosevelt no longer lived in the White House.